enjoy
book!
Joanne

Shadowed Remembrances

Joanne M. Kerzmann

PublishAmerica
Baltimore

First printing

ISBN: 1-4137-1904-X

PUBLISHED BY PUBLISHAMERICA, LLLP

www.publishamerica.com

Baltimore

Printed in the United States of America

*Dedicated to Mom and Dave
for supporting me in my endeavors
and always being there for me
AND John,
I love you and am so thankful
that God gave me a man
who believes in me
and my dream to write.*

Thank you to my sister, Lori;
if you had not given me that one last push,
I would have given up.

AND Thank you to my Lord God,
who has given me this dream to write
and blessed me beyond all that
I could ask for or imagine.

Prologue

The little girl tossed under the covers, restless and disturbed. A chill wind blew inside the open window, swaying the curtains. She leaned her sleeping face into the pillow and exhaled a soft breath.

Please don't hurt me, a voice cried downstairs. *No!* The shot woke the girl from her sleep. She pulled on her robe, her body cold and shaking. She walked out to the hallway and peeked through the railing. *No*, she gasped. She wanted to cry but fear silenced her. Her fingers clutched the white railing so hard that the blood drained from her skin. Her heart pounded.

"Oh my, God," she heard her father moan; he held his wife in his arms, rocking her bloodied body. The girl saw the black gun pointed at her father's head. *No, not Daddy. Jesus, please help us.* She held her hand over her mouth to keep from crying out.

"No," her daddy shouted, "why are you doing this?"

The intruder, void of sympathy, aimed the gun at the child's father.

"Because you got in the way." He pulled the trigger. The shot rang out so loud in the girl's ears. She sucked in her breath as she saw her daddy fall to the floor. She heard him cry out her name and then said no more.

The girl stood up, wanting so desperately to run down and wake her mommy and daddy. She needed them. She touched the railing and turned quickly; she couldn't let the man with the gun see her.

The girl ran into her room and hid under her bed. She covered her ears with shaking hands and huddled there, so frightened. *Oh God. please don't let him find me. Please save me.* She tried to stifle her sobs. The door to her room creaked open. She sucked in her breath. He came in. *Please go away.*

The man with the gun swept through her room and turned around. He left almost as quickly as he came in. But the girl lay still in the room, shaking and holding her ears for a long time after the man left.

Chapter One

Detective Torianna Silverman stood inside room twenty-two in *Joe's Motel*. Another crime scene investigation, the third one this week, in the same neighborhood. Detective Silverman, armed with notepad in hand, made a rough sketch of the surroundings. Mahoney took the measurements of the room for her. Johnson, at the moment, was taking pictures from all angles of the room.

Detective Silverman nearly jumped out of her skin when she heard the voice behind her. "I'm sorry, Detective, I didn't mean to frighten you."

Sure you didn't, Torianna thought impatiently, *every time I'm busy, you have to come poking your nose around.*

"What is it, Simmons? I'm kind of busy right now."

"I see that," Detective Simmons said, as he edged closer to her, looking at her notepad.

"Shouldn't you be out trying to find the guy who did this?" she replied a little too harshly. Even she regretted her tone.

"I'm waiting for your team to finish and fill us in on what we're looking for."

She smiled. "That's good. Then you'll let me get back to work." She turned abruptly and spoke quietly to Mahoney.

Detective Simmons got the hint and left the motel room. "Simmons bothering you again?"

She looked up from her sketch, not wanting to think about Detective Simmons. "It's no trouble. I can handle him."

Mahoney shrugged and went back to his task.

Detective Silverman walked over to the victim, sprawled out on the floor. Torianna shuddered involuntarily at the sight of the still body. She looked so young. Detective Silverman had seen many corpses since she joined the crime scene division, but the sight of a lifeless body still affected her. "She had her whole life ahead of her," Torianna whispered.

She bent down and watched the EMT gather his equipment and move out of the way for the Medical Examiner. There was no need for the EMT now; the ME moved in, preparing to pronounce the victim dead. Detective Silverman watched carefully practiced hands moved over the body, mechanically checking for non-existent vital signs.

* * *

Torianna sat on the weight bench, sweat trickling down from under her headband. She brought her arms together as if trying to hurt someone. The fierceness in her eyes and the way she huffed brought Phillip's head up. He looked at Torianna and wondered at her angry demeanor. He almost walked over to her to see if she wanted his help, but she let go of the machine, making the forty pound weight bang down. She stood up and grabbed her towel, wiping the sweat from her forehead.

Phillip stood up, laying his copy of the *Wall Street Journal* on the coffee table. He turned to look at her, a question in his eyes. She dared him to question her. He simply dropped his arms at his sides and looked helplessly at her.

"I'm taking a shower."

Phillip walked into the kitchen to make her some tea. He heard Torianna turn the shower on. He knew just how she liked it. Steaming hot. The hissing kettle startled him. As he reached for the cabinet to get a teacup, he noticed the answering machine light blinking. He wondered why Torianna never checked her messages.

He pressed the rewind button. *Silverman, it's Mahoney. The ME finished the autopsy on the Jensen girl. You might find it interesting. Call me when you get a chance.* Phillip hit the stop button harder than he wanted to. "I hate her job," he grumbled.

10

He carried her teacup to the bathroom expecting the door to be unlocked. He put the tea on a table in the hallway. He knocked lightly. "Tori, honey, are you okay? I brought you some tea."

There was no answer.

He knocked a little harder. "Please, honey, open up the door. I want to see if you're alright."

"I'm fine," Tori snapped.

Phillip swallowed his hasty reply, not wanting to upset her anymore. "I'll leave your tea on the table here. Hurry out before it starts to cool off." His response met with silence. "I'm going to head home. Please call me in the morning." His voice held a pleading note.

Phillip shook his head and listened to the shower. He touched the wooden door with his left palm. He said good night and left the apartment.

Inside the bathroom steam enveloped everything, the mirror, the toilet seat cover, everywhere. Torianna rested her palms on the wet tiles and leaned into the shower. The hot water ran over her head, drenching her short red hair. It ran down her back, washing over her skin. She grabbed the bar of soap and lathered her face, washing it. She leaned under the water and rinsed the lather then slammed the faucet into place, shutting the water off. She reached for the towel and patted herself dry.

After slipping into her robe, she walked out of the bathroom and picked up the tea Phillip left on the table. A tear rolled down her cheek when she thought of how she treated Phillip. She wanted to call him but had no energy.

She took a sip of the lukewarm tea and then put the cup in the microwave to reheat it. Absently, she pressed the play button on her answering machine. "The autopsy," she spoke to the empty room, "find it interesting?" She sighed and picked up the phone. Without thought, she dialed Mahoney's number. His wife answered.

"Hi, Sherry, it's Tori, can I speak to John?"

"Sure, just a minute."

"Well, Silverman, I thought you'd never call."

"I was busy with other things."

"Ooh, I guess Phillip was there."

"That's none of your business, Mahoney, besides, is that any way to talk to a lady."

"You're not like most ladies, Silverman."

"I don't know if that's a compliment or an insult."

"It's a compliment."

Torianna passed over his banter. "So, what's up?"

"The ME found the same entry wound as the other two murders."

"That's what you called to tell me?"

"Yeah, but it's interesting."

Torianna cut him off. "I know, Mahoney. It's almost a certainty now that the perp is the same for each case. Look at our other evidence. But you're forgetting one important piece of information."

"What's that?"

"I'm going on vacation for two weeks. Remember?"

"Oh yeah. Well, I guess that leaves me in charge"

"Guess so."

"So why'd you call? You didn't have to."

"I don't know. Maybe I just wanted to hear your voice." She laughed.

"Watch it, little lady, I'm a married man."

"I know, I know." She grew quiet. "Goodnight, Mahoney. See ya in two weeks.

"Hurry back."

* * *

"Mr. Torrence, Miss. Silverman is here."

Phillip nodded from his hunched position at his desk; he was in the middle of important negotiations for this business merger. He smiled and waved Torianna into his office. She sat and watched him talk on the phone. Worried about her news she had to tell, especially after the way she acted last night, Torianna sat erect, waiting. After a few minutes, he was off the phone.

"How are you today?"

"Fine. I guess."

"You've been under a lot of stress lately."

"You've switched professions? Taking up psychology?"

"No. I'm just worried about you, that's all." He came around his desk and sat on the chair next to her. He took her hand in his and smiled at her. "I can't wait to go on this trip with you."

Torianna heard the excitement in his voice and stood up quickly, distancing herself from him. "That's what I need to talk to you about."

Phillip's heart beat faster as he noticed her serious tone.

"I don't want you to go on the trip with me."

"Excuse me?"

"That didn't sound very good, did it?"

"No." Phillip wasn't smiling.

"I need some time alone."

"Alone? I don't think you should be alone now."

"You don't think I should be alone? You don't need to do my thinking for me. I'm a big girl."

"Tori, that's not what I meant. I want to help you."

"Then let me go by myself."

"But what about all the plans? I canceled my business trip to Paris."

"Now you can go to Paris. You'll be happier there, than with me."

"No I won't. You know how I feel about you."

"No." She sat down and stared at his desk, hoping to hear the telephone ring and interrupt their conversation.

Phillip wanted to hold Torianna, but he stopped himself, not wanting to push her further away. He knew how she shut down emotionally to any physical touch when she was upset or annoyed. Touching her now would just fuel her fire. He stared at her finger, seeing the diamond reflect the light in his office. He remembered the night he proposed four months ago. With some time off from her caseload, Torianna had agreed to visit his parents in Upstate New York. It took a lot of coaxing to get her to come. After dinner, he asked her. The lightly falling snow made that Valentine's Day special, adding a sense of romance to the evening.

Torianna abruptly removed her hand from her lap and the shimmering diamond disappeared. Startled by her quick movement, Phillip came back to the present.

Torianna reached out unexpectedly and caressed his smooth cheek. Phillip covered her soft hand with his. He saw tears form in Torianna's eyes. "Please trust me, Phillip. I need this."

He looked down, but still held her hand close to his face. "I do trust you, Tori. Please tell me you know that by now."

Torianna sniffed back her tears and stood quickly. "I have to go." She walked out the door without looking back.

Chapter Two

High in the clear sky, the sun warmed Agatha as she knelt in her garden. She deftly pulled up the weeds surrounding her rhododendrons and miniature spruce trees. She broke the hardened ground with her hand rake and began digging a hole for her new addition, a pink azalea bush. She stuck her gloved hand in the hole and cleared out the loose dirt. She reached behind her and took the azalea bush out of its planter and smiled. She loved flowers. Her aching back kept her from planting more flowers and bushes in her yard. *Such a big yard,* she sighed, *and I'm getting too old to tend it.*

Brushing her thoughts away as easily as they entered her mind, Agatha settled the azalea bush firmly in the ground. She poured some water from her watering pail and then dumped the dark rich soil into the hole. She patted it down and poured some more water over the dirt. *I really should get some wood chips to cover the dirt, to keep the weeds out. Oh, well, maybe when there's more time.*

Agatha leaned back and sat on the grass, not caring if her gardening dress got dirty. She wiped her arm across her forehead and looked up into the sky, her straw hat shading her eyes from the sun's hot rays. It was such a beautiful day.

"Aggie, Aggie," a voice called from the front of her house.

Agatha smiled towards her visitor. "I'm back here, Jonas, by the rock garden."

By the time Jonas reached his neighbor, he felt winded, his cheeks were flushed and his thinning white hair was flying up haphazardly. Agatha knew Jonas and this frequent state of disarray which settled

15

over him; she hid her smile and got ready for a little chat with her old friend. When in this frame of mind, Jonas never let her get a word in the conversation.

"Oh, I'm so glad you're here, Aggie."

About to ask where else she would be, she caught herself and let him continue.

"I've had it with the Whitfield boys playing ball in the street. I tried to be nice about it and not say anything, but they've gone too far this time."

Agatha gave him the inquiring nod he needed. "They broke my window, Aggie." She gasped at the right spot and then he said, "That's not all. Then when I ran out of the house chasing them away, the boys ran over my begonias and tulips. They're crushed now."

"Ohh," Agatha let out a low sigh.

"Aggie, will you be serious. You may be next. I chased those boys away. Now they may come down this end of the street. And you better watch out…your windows and flowers."

Agatha decided to end his tirade there. "Come on, Jonas, let's go inside and get some iced tea."

"But, what about…"

"Everything's going to be all right. Did you talk to the boys' parents? I'm sure Mr. and Mrs. Whitfield will be willing to pay for the damages."

"No, I haven't talked to their parents. I guess I should."

"Now that's more like it. I've got some blueberry muffins fresh from the oven. Your favorite." Agatha walked Jonas into her screened-in porch towards the waiting muffins and iced tea.

* * *

Nick Keyes sat down in his chair and exhaled loudly. Another hectic day and still no help. As the elected County Coroner, Nick oversaw the medical and legal investigation of death. His little niche in the world, carved out in a small Pennsylvania town, remained undisturbed until now. Previously, he served as the town's only funeral director. At first he loved the idea of being the County Coroner; however, the fantasy was wearing off.

It seemed as if Nick's young Deputy Coroner knew three times as much as he did. Nick felt no career competition with her. He did not have a big ego. His problem arose when Sheila, his deputy, decided to get married, leaving him without a forensic specialist. This was the worst time, because his caseload had begun to triple.

Nick stood up from his chair and walked across the room. He reached into a pail of hot soapy water and grabbed a sponge. He drained the sponge of excess water so that it would not run through the holes in the autopsy table. He ran the sponge over the cold metal and wished he could go home to bed.

* * *

As quietly as possible, her fingers flew over the keyboard making fluid taping noises. He must not hear her. The words on the monitor quickly took the shape of her focused thoughts. *What to do with the disc?* That was still a question nagging at her brain.

She knew this information needed to get into the right hands, foiling his plans. She tried focusing her mind on the task at hand. Her breathing once again grew calm and her fingers flew over the keyboard.

She had mixed a sedative in his wine after dinner, nothing harmful, just enough of a dose to keep him sleeping soundly. *If he found me at the computer...* She left that thought hang heavy on her mind.

She grew tired after sitting erect at the desk chair for over an hour. *Enough for tonight,* she thought. She saved the information and took the disc out of the drive. She quickly exited out of the program, completed her session, and shut the monitor and computer off. She made sure that everything in his office lay exactly as she found it when she entered. If he found one pencil out of place, he would know someone had been at his desk. *So meticulous and organized. A perfectionist. Too much of a perfectionist, for my taste.* She held the disc firmly in her hand, not wanting to lose it now, not when her work neared a close.

* * *

Agatha sat at her desk and checked her bank statement once more, her calculations not adding up correctly. Either she or the bank had made a mistake. She hit the clear button on her calculator and punched in the numbers again, trying to make sense of this nonsense.

After some minutes, she sat back in despair. *Well, I guess the bank's right.* She tried to remain calm, but knew no escape. Ever since Charlie died, things went wrong. First, the septic tank needed draining; it cost her a small fortune. Then the refrigerator broke down. She needed one, so she bought a new one on credit, something out of the ordinary for her. *Come on, you old fusspot,* she chided herself, *pull yourself together. Tori and her young man are coming to visit tomorrow and you can't let them see what's really going on here. They have worries enough of their own.*

Agatha leaned back in her chair and rubbed her weary eyes. Always the hopeful one, she smiled and let out a breath, speaking softly, "Everything's going to turn out all right. It always does."

She got up and stretched her aching back. She walked to her night stand and reached for the bottle of aspirin. She needed two or her back wouldn't let her sleep tonight. She swallowed the pills and drank some of the water from her glass.

Already in her nightgown, she pulled back her covers and sat down on the bed. Taking off her slippers, she laid back and sighed. After today's hard work of gardening and putting up with Jonas, she relished the comfortable feel of her bed. For a single moment, Agatha wished for the arms of her dear husband to comfort her, but he was rejoicing with the Lord in Heaven now.

She reached for her Bible and opened to where her bookmark rested in the Psalms. Reading through the Psalms amazed Agatha; such truths were found there. She ended her day with Psalm 15, her favorite words to live by.

* * *

Nick tried to open his door awkwardly balancing three bags of groceries and his keys. Forgetting to leave the light on outside his front door, he fumbled in the dark. As he almost reached his point of frustration, the key seemed to fit perfectly into the hole.

He opened the door, tripping over a black figure on the floor. "Smoky!" he yelled. "Do you have to sleep right in the hallway? One of these days you're gonna make me fall and break my neck. And who's gonna bury me, huh?" He laughed, not getting any reaction out of his canine friend.

"What are you looking at? Come help me put these groceries away before I drop them. I got you some food."

The bulky sheepdog rushed into the kitchen after his master getting in the middle of every step Nick tried to take. Barely making it to the kitchen table, Nick deposited his packages and leaned against the counter. He reached into the refrigerator and opened a can of soda. Pink tongue hanging out of his mouth, Smoky stood watching his master quietly waiting for his dinner.

"Okay, here you go." Nick started to take the groceries out of the bags and found the can of dog food near the top. He poured the food into Smoky's dish and watched him wolf the meat down.

"You know, you act as if I never feed you."

Nick smiled and began to empty the rest of his bags. He finished and walked out of the kitchen towards the bathroom. After today's work, he needed a hot shower.

After his shower, Smoky met him at the door wanting to play. Nick gave in and tossed a chewed-up bone across the living room floor. *Something Lynn always hated,* he thought wryly. He played with his dog for a bit and relished the quiet. It felt good not to get "the call." More and more each day he hated this job of having to go to the crime scene and making the initial medical examination. But it was his job, and he had to do it, for now at least.

* * *

The woman still held the disc firmly in her hand. She wanted to hide it somewhere different tonight. She changed its hiding place many times, just in case his suspicions arose.

She stood by the door and watched him sleep. She watched the wind blow softly through the open window, rustling the lace curtains. She saw his profile lighted by the soft glow of the moon. His right arm rested over to her side of the bed, the place where she should be now. She stood watching him sleep; sometimes he was restless, but not tonight. She gave him a different sedative in his drink earlier. She wanted him to stay out of her way while she finished her work.

The woman finally felt relaxed and decided to hide the disc in the pocket of her winter coat, tucked way in the back of her walk-in closet. She sighed contentedly after safely depositing the disc and tip-toed across the cold wood floor onto the Persian rug. She pulled back the satin sheets and slowly sat down on the bed gingerly shifting her weight on the mattress. Her husband shifted in his sleep and moved his heavy arm away from her pillow. Grateful, the woman pulled the covers up and moved to the farthest side of the bed away from his immediate grasp.

Chapter Three

Torianna hit the steering wheel, grumbling; cars waited at a standstill, for over an hour. The sound of a construction crew at work reverberated down the highway. Torianna grabbed her cup from the holder and drank the warm soda. She smiled weakly down at her tabby cat, Prints, and he purred under her soft attention as her hand rubbed under his furry neck. Torianna called her feisty little pet "Prints" because of his annoying habit of getting into her potted plant, no longer a fixture of her apartment, and walking all over her carpets and table getting paw prints everywhere. It was either the cat or the plant. She chose the cat. Whenever someone asked his name, she answered, "Prints" and they thought she said, "Prince." After too many times to remember, Torianna stopped correcting people. *Well,* Torianna thought ruefully, *you are my little prince, aren't you?* Prints stretched out on her front seat and yawned, agreeing with her.

About to reach for her cup again, a horn startled her from behind. Cars started to move. She settled back into driving position and shifted out of neutral into first gear. The traffic started off at a snail's pace. Torianna, known for her fast driving, passed a slow driver and eased into the fast lane. She pictured Phillip sitting there in Prints' place, telling her the hazards of driving too fast. She always humored him, but felt a little freer with him not with her telling her to slow down. She relaxed in the flow of traffic and fiddled with the radio trying to tune in a good song.

* * *

The man closed the phone booth door. The noise of the passing car made hearing hard.

"Do you think she knows?"

The man inside the booth laughed off the other man's statement. "Are you serious? She doesn't even know where I've been when I come home from work with someone else's perfume on."

The other man grew more serious. "Do you really think this is something to laugh about it? She might know something."

"Listen to me, I know what I'm doing. And I suggest you leave the little lady out of it. If she gets too nosy, which she won't, I'll deal with her."

The man seemed disgruntled, but ceased to argue. "Fine. I'll let you deal with her. But if anything goes wrong, don't say I didn't warn you."

"Stop worrying. Nothing will go wrong."

"All right. I gotta go. My boss just came in. I have a meeting."

"Fine. I'll call you."

* * *

As Torianna drove across the bridge, she peeked over the edge and saw the Delaware River flowing below. She smiled. It felt good going home to Pennsylvania. She hadn't been back to visit in such a long time.

Phillip had planned this trip. He wanted to meet her grandmother and he thought the visit would do Torianna some good. *And now he's not even here.* She tried not to think about Phillip. Not yet, at least. She had two weeks for thoughts about him and their relationship. Right now, she was itching to see her grandmother.

She paid the toll and rolled up her window, easing into the two lane highway which brought her to Pennsylvania. She rubbed Prints' head, special attention that he loved. Phillip offered to watch her cat, but she wanted to take him with her, a constant faithful companion.

The rest of the twenty-mile stretch of route 80 west went by in silence. She turned off her radio and watched the familiar

22

surroundings zoom past her car windows. She felt her stomach tighten and wondered at her anxiety.

Torianna never admitted this to Phillip, but she felt relieved that he suggested this trip. Her workload weighed heavily on her lately. She wasn't sure how much more she would be able to take without a rest. Captain Elway approved her vacation plans and wished her a nice rest. She welcomed the reprieve from Detective Simmons. She seemed to run into him at every possible turn at the station. Not fearful of him, Torianna simply became annoyed at his lewd remarks and irksome behavior.

Before she knew it, the highway split and Torianna drove for another few miles then got off on her exit.

The white house came into her sights and Torianna shivered involuntarily. The house evoked a sorrow deep within her and she stifled the teardrop threatening to fall. She would not cry. She would not remember. She had a sudden desire to turn around and ride back to her apartment and her work.

The front door opened and Agatha peeked her head out. She clapped her hands together and dropped the dishcloth she held. She ran to Torianna's car. Hiding the sorrow evoked by memories, Torianna rubbed Prints' head and got out of the car. Her grandmother met her with a welcoming hug.

She sniffed her tears away, "Where's Phillip?"

Torianna disengaged herself from her grandmother's arms and turned away, fumbling with her bags in the trunk. "He's not with me."

"Oh, but why not, dear?"

"We thought, well, I thought it would be best."

"I don't understand."

Unprepared for this barrage of questions, Torianna hedged. "Everything's fine. I just wanted some time alone and," she added, "I get you all to myself."

Agatha decided not to press the matter with her granddaughter. She bustled about helping her with the bags and led Torianna into the house.

* * *

Torianna turned restlessly in her bed. She kept tossing, not able to get to sleep. A strong wind blew up against the window. Torianna feared closing her eyes, because a dark figure haunted her sleep.

She grew impatient with her fitful state of unrest and threw the covers back, laying in the darkness and chiding herself for feeling scared. She got out of bed and put her slippers on, pulling her robe around her cold body.

She opened the door to her bedroom and entered the hallway. Darkness met her eyes, lit only by a small nightlight in the hallway. She tripped over something on the floor. When she bent down to examine the object, her face came close to the railing. Her hands, larger than so long ago, hesitantly touched the white railing. She pulled away, as if the wood burned her. She leaned back from the railing and remembered.

Her fingers clutched the railing so hard. Her knuckles turned white. She recalled how her heart pounded and what she prayed. *"No, not Daddy too. Jesus please help us."*

"Who are you talking to?"

Torianna jumped up, shaking, "Grandma?"

"Well, who'd you think I was?"

"Nobody. I mean, oh, nothing."

"What were you whispering?"

"Nothing." She turned away, not wanting to answer.

Agatha reached out to her granddaughter and tried to comfort her, wanting to help. Torianna pulled away slightly, not able to speak about the past right then.

"I'm gonna get some milk."

"Are you going to be okay?"

Helplessly she responded, "Sure, I'm fine."

Agatha watched her granddaughter's hasty exit.

* * *

A few hours after her encounter with Torianna, Agatha tossed on her bed. She opened her eyes to the darkness, watching the wind through the windows and the bending oak branches. She looked around the room, only forms of the furniture visible. Not wanting to turn the light on, she was relaxed in the peaceful atmosphere. She yearned for her granddaughter to feel the same peace she felt. She closed her eyes in whispered supplication to the Lord.

Chapter Four

The woman awakened from a fretful sleep, her body shaking and drenched with sweat; the nightmare haunted her again. She glanced across the bed, seeing her husband's place empty. The woman's grogginess dissipated a survival mechanism. She needed her wits about her to survive.

She stretched her hand across his side of the bed; it was cold and the sheet was unwrinkled. *He must have been up for some time already,* she surmised, a worried frown creasing her brow. *I have to get up. I can't let him find me here.*

She tugged her silk robe off the chair and settled her feet in her slippers. Starting to walk out of the bedroom, she stopped suddenly remembering the disc. *I'll come back for it later. I don't know why I'm getting so anxious.*

The woman progressed cautiously down the hall; the moon was beginning to set and the sun wanted to rise. Darkness still surrounded. She disliked walking around her house at night, especially since she found out... *What's that?* She heard a slight creaking of the floor behind her. When she turned, emptiness met her.

Her heart pounded; she fought hard to control it. She entered the kitchen and walked towards the refrigerator door. She poured herself a glass of orange juice and then heard his voice, cold and calculating, behind her.

"I would put that glass down if I were you." The woman's hand trembled slightly, sloshing orange juice onto the counter.

"What do you want?"

"I found out what you're doing."

Stalling, she answered, "I have no idea what you're talking about. I just got out of bed to get something to drink. I couldn't sleep."

"Sure, my darling, but you know what I'm talking about." He waited for a response. "I found the disc in my office."

She stiffened her heart cold, angry. *He'll get away with this.* But then she heard a voice inside her head, saying *Vengeance is mine.* "Yes, I do know what you've done, but I'm not afraid of you anymore." She hoped her voice belied the fear she felt.

"It looks like no one will ever know what's happened." He flashed his .357 Magnum in front of her. She cringed and he sneered, "So you see, no one will ever know."

Her spirit fought, grasping to hold on to life. "Wait, please, you don't want to do this."

"Really? You leave me no choice. You got in the way, my dear. I didn't want to have to kill you."

"You don't. I'll leave and not say anything. I promise."

"I'm sorry. I can't let you do that."

A tear escaped her wide eyes, her pent up emotion spilling out. "You won't get away with this."

He grabbed her small body with his gloved hands and stuck the gun in her hand. She struggled, but he held on tightly from behind. His hot, tepid breath on her neck sickened her. For my plan to work, you're going to have to shoot yourself."

She gasped, wiggling. She reached out, trying to grab onto something. Her hand touched the refrigerator door. The cool surface steadied her. He pulled her away. "Stop struggling. There's no use in that. It's all over for you. Why not go out with a little dignity."

She cringed under his fierce words. *God, help me. Don't let him get away with this.*

He grabbed her right hand and made her point the magnum at her temple. He whispered in her ear. "Bye, sweetheart." He forced her finger onto the trigger and fired the weapon. The woman slumped in his arms. He tried to keep her head off his chest, not wanting any blood stains on his clothes; however, the scant spattering of blood on his dark shirt escaped his notice. The man carried the dead body of his wife a few feet away and laid her on the floor, face down. He laid the magnum a foot away from her limp hand. Not affected by the sight of her blood, he stared down for a few minutes and said, "You should've left things alone."

He pulled the note out of his coat pocket and laid it on the table. Her *suicide* note. He had to make this look as real as possible.

* * *

Nick got the call at 2:00 am. He rolled over in bed, startled by the loud ringing. He knew he would never get used to these bizarre hours. *Why can't people kill each other at a more reasonable hour,* he grumbled as he answered Officer Devon's call. He sat up in bed. This was no everyday occurrence. The Mayor's wife was dead. Nick mumbled that he'd be right over.

The Mayor's wife? I just saw her at the grocery store yesterday. She appeared fine. He slipped into his faded jeans, the nearest piece of apparel at his reach and pulled a T-shirt over his head. *This is just great! How am I supposed to handle this without Sheila? Cool down, big guy.* He tried giving himself a pep talk. *You're gonna do just fine. You're not exactly ignorant in this area. You've seen enough dead bodies before.* He whispered a short prayer for help.

He raced around the room. Shoes. Of all the times to lose them. Nick bent down and searched underneath his bed. Smoky chose that moment to come into the room carrying his chewed-up, saliva-covered bone. He nudged Nick in the rear, with his wet nose. "Not now, Smoky, I've got some important business to attend to." He scratched Smoky's ears and promised to play later.

* * *

The scene that met his eye when he walked into the house amazed Nick. *The Mayor is living it up. Maybe I should run for mayor and raise the taxes.* "There you are, Keyes," Chief Roberts called, motioning Nick forward. Nick edged closer in between the commotion of uniformed officers and detectives in the living room. He remembered Sheila telling him once to limit the number of officers milling about the crime scene. Too many hands could lead to destroying important evidence. Chief Roberts interrupted his thoughts.

"What took you so long?"

"Couldn't find my shoes, Sir."

"Oh," the Chief chuckled as he led Nick towards the kitchen. He stifled his laughter when he came to the crime scene. Nick raised his head to see over the taller officers, hating his short stature. The Chief cleared the way and ushered Nick into the room. They both knelt down next to the victim.

"She's all yours. I'll send the EMT in here to help with transporting the body when you're ready." The Chief left Nick alone with the corpse. Nick assumed that the Ident officer finished collecting evidence and photographing the body, so he began his initial examination, making a few notes in his ever-present notepad. He pronounced the Mayor's wife dead at 2:45 am, the legal time of death, not sure yet of the actual time of death.

He called the EMT into the room to prepare the corpse for transport to the morgue. The Chief met him in the hallway. "I think it's a suicide." He waited for Nick to answer.

"I don't know, Sir. I can't give you a definitive answer until I do the autopsy."

"Oh, cut the crap, Nick, you know she shot herself. Look at the evidence."

"I understand, Sir, but I really need to get back to the lab and start the autopsy."

Chief Roberts let his officer leave the house. He hoped this case ended soon, without a scandal; a scandal was not exactly what the town needed right then. Besides, he'd always liked Sherry and it was a shame what happened to her.

* * *

Nick stepped outside, gulping in the fresh air, relieved they found the body not too long after her death. Nick carefully walked to his car; it was getting dark, with a thick fog settling in.

He stepped down the path to the driveway, almost near his car, when he noticed a small object at his feet. He bent down, picking it up. *A rubber glove.* He held the glove with the tips of his fingers. *If Sheila was here, she'd yell at me for not wearing gloves.* He could get his prints over the prints on the glove, smudging them. *Anyway, what am I thinking? Who said this glove is evidence.*

He turned the glove over and saw a smear of blood on the index finger. *Isn't this interesting?* Nick held the glove gingerly between his index finger and thumb and crossed the short distance to his car, in search of a bag to hold the glove for evidence. Evidence of what? Not sure yet, his instinct told him to guard this glove.

He shifted into gear and backed out of the long driveway. As he stayed in second gear driving forward, he realized for the first time the length of this driveway, secluding the Mayor's house from prying eyes.

* * *

At the lab several hours later, Nick mustered the courage to start the autopsy. He knew this case called for a medical-legal autopsy since he considered suicide a possible cause of death and a ruling for legal purposes would be required. He almost picked up the phone and dialed Sheila's number. Performing his first solo autopsy, he sorely missed Sheila's expertise.

Here goes nothing. He looked over at the still-clothed corpse lying on the cold metal table. He identified the body and assigned a number to the toe tag. He grabbed the lab camera and photographed the body. As he then proceeded to undress the corpse, he wondered how long he was going to have this job. He took the camera and photographed the naked corpse, skin waxy in appearance, a blue-gray color; the lips and nails were pale. The body was cool to the touch. Nick noted the fixed lividity and he touched the skin, no apparent blanching with the pressure. He observed more advanced rigor mortis; the corneas of her eyes were clouded. Nick estimated she'd been dead for at least six to eight hours.

He then weighed, measured and x-rayed the body. As he worked over the corpse, he suddenly remembered the absence of the Mayor at his house during the search. He wondered if the Mayor found his wife's body. *What a tough break. Such a nice couple. Never would've thought there were problems.*

He finished the external examination and then proceeded to perform the toxicology test. He prepared for the internal examination where a body-length "Y" incision would open the entire front of the corpse. His hands trembled slightly, then he regained his control. *I've made it this far, I can finish.*

He removed all the organs with painstaking concentration and weighed them on the scale to the right of the table. He examined the genitals and uterus for any sign of pregnancy or sexual assault. With an intermastoid incision, he cut the skull away and removed and examined the brain.

He removed the bullet lodged in her skull and placed it in a plastic bag for ballistics evidence. Nick returned the organs to the body cavities and stitched the "Y" incision. He still had work ahead of him with preparing the autopsy protocol. Nick turned away from the corpse and went to get some coffee.

Chapter Five

Torianna sat up in bed stretching her arms over her head. She leaned back and saw her grandmother's Bible on her bedside table. She smiled. Her grandmother never was very subtle. She took the worn Bible in hand and opened to the bookmark. She wondered if her grandmother left the place marked for her or if she had been reading from this passage herself.

Torianna opened to Hebrews chapter 11. Agatha scribbled *Hall of Faith* in the margin. She began to read about the faithful men and women of God.

Now faith is being sure of what you hope for and certain of what you do not see. Torianna read the first verse Agatha highlighted and she whispered a hurried prayer to experience such a faith.

The tantalizing smell of frying bacon wafted up the stairs and Torianna got out of bed to get dressed. Suddenly hungry, she remembered her grandmother's delicious home-cooking; her stomach urged her downstairs. Torianna entered the kitchen and sat down at the table, waiting for her grandmother to notice her. Engrossed in checking the muffins and the frying bacon, Agatha did not hear her granddaughter come in.

"Oh, Tori, dear, you're up. I knew the smell of my bacon would get you out of bed." She came over to Tori and gave her a hug. "Feeling better, I hope."

"What do you mean?"

"You know, you seemed a little bit distracted when I saw you last night in the hallway."

"Oh, that. It was nothing." She took a bite of an apple. "I guess I just wasn't used to such a strange bed."

"I don't think that bed's so strange. You used to sleep in it when you were a little girl."

"I know that, Grandma," Tori defended herself.

"Well," Agatha tried changing the subject as she expertly managed to turn the bacon and prepare Tori's muffin, "what are you going to do today?"

"I'm not sure. Maybe go for a walk. See some old friends." She took another bite of her apple. "I haven't seen my friends from high school in a long time. Do you know if any of them are still living in town?"

"I know Nick is," Agatha turned a sly smile on her granddaughter.

Torianna blushed, knowing full well why her grandmother gave her such a look. "That's nice," she tried to sound uninterested, focusing her attention on the half-eaten apple in her hand.

"So, are you going to see him?" Agatha prompted.

"Why would I want to do that?" she asked.

"You both used to be pretty close."

"That's history. Besides, it wouldn't be appropriate for me to see him. He's married, you know."

Agatha almost dropped the plate she carried to the table.

"What's wrong?"

"Nothing dear, I just thought you knew."

"Knew what?"

"About Lynn."

"What aren't you telling me, Grandma?"

She set the plate in front of Torianna. "She passed away three years ago."

"Three years," Torianna's words trailed off. "I haven't seen Nick since the wedding. I had no idea."

"Of course you had no idea. Now look what I've done. Spoiled your day before it got started."

Torianna ignored her grandmother's fretting. "Grandma, how did...what happened?"

"A car accident by the bridge. It was a bad night to be out. Raining so hard, so slippery. Such a shame." Torianna stared at her, not knowing why she had trouble accepting this fact. She had seen so much death lately, almost more than she could handle. "Now eat the food before it gets cold."

Torianna felt like a little girl again, listening to her grandmother tell her what to do. Somehow, she felt comforted. Underneath her tough exterior, she was still that little girl who missed her mother and father and had to grow up without them.

"Maybe I'll go see him."

"He's the county coroner now."

"But Nick's a funeral director. What does he know about...."

"He's doing the best job he can, especially since his deputy coroner up and married on him."

"Oh." Torianna remained silent for a moment. "How do you know so much about Nick?"

"I see him at church."

Torianna avoided her grandmother's steady gaze and ate her breakfast in silence. This conversation was getting too close to the past and she did not want her grandmother to see that she was the least bit interested in seeing Nick again.

* * *

Nick sat at his desk absorbed in completing his final opinion about the autopsy he performed. His back ached and his head throbbed. He felt trapped inside this lab and he needed some air. He decided to take a break as soon as he finished the autopsy protocol. He made a note to make sure he developed the photographs of the corpse to include them in the case file. Nick looked at the death certificate where he filled in the manner of death. "Deceased shot self." He felt unsure labeling the death a suicide. All the evidence pointed to suicide; the suicide note, the gun found near the body, the bullet wound to the temple, which showed a rim of burn from the flame caused by a near contact shot, with the gun held less than one inch from the body. Nick conducted a trace metal test on the victim's right hand. The results showed that she held the revolver in a normal suicide position. But it still felt wrong.

The glove. That's it. Nick leaned back in his chair and exhaled loudly. *This was not good. I never should have taken the glove. The Ident Technician should have taken it as evidence. But what was it doing away from the crime scene.* Nick thought about what to do. Get it tested then hand it over as potential evidence. *I should do that quickly*, he thought. He leaned so far back in his chair, with his feet up on the desk, that the wheels rolled and the chair fell back. He landed on the floor, the chair breaking his fall. His knees bent, still laid on the floor, he saw someone leaning over him. *Sheila?*

The person leaned closer, but Nick's bright desk light shining in his face made visibility impossible. He shaded his eyes with his hand and the person got the hint, moving the light away.

The woman reached out her hand and helped him up. She steadied him and burst into laughter.

Nick raised his eyebrows. He saw no humor in the situation.

"It was funny."

"Excuse me?" Nick said

"When you fell, I saw the whole thing."

"I'm so happy I was able to give you some entertainment for the morning."

Torianna chuckled. *Morning? What has he been sniffing! I better get him out of this lab.* "Morning? It's more like six o'clock in the evening."

Nick opened his eyes wide in attention.

"How long have you been cooped up here?"

Nick rubbed his sore head, thankful he hadn't damaged any body parts. "Since early this morning, I guess. The time must have slipped by."

"I guess so."

Nick tried to recall any appointments on his schedule today. His mind drawing a blank, he wondered why a beautiful woman stood in his morgue. In his befuddled state, he noticed the woman showed no signs of possibly fainting from such close proximity to dead bodies.

Understanding Nick's confusion, Torianna moved forward and offered her hand. "I can see you don't remember me."

Nick focused on the woman's face, not sure what to say. *I must have hit my head pretty hard. I can't even think of anything to say to this beautiful woman. That's never happened to me before. This lab work's getting to me.*

Clasping Nick's hand, Torianna introduced herself. "Torianna Silverman."

Nick's mouth gaped open, but he quickly hid his surprise. "This is quite unexpected, Tori...I can still call you that, can't I?"

Torianna smiled. "Sure. How have you been?"

"Pretty good."

Torianna interrupted him, "You're still holding my hand."

"Oh, yeah." The diamond on her finger reflected the light, catching Nick's attention. He held more firmly onto her hand and grinned. "So," he examined the ring, "who's the rock from?"

Torianna disengaged her hand from his grasp. "This 'rock' is from my fiancé, Phillip."

Nick turned and sat down; holding out his hand, he offered her a seat by his desk. "On vacation?"

"Yes."

"I have to meet Phillip."

"I guess that's gonna have to wait. He's not here."

"I know he's not here, but at your grandmother's...that is where you're staying, isn't it?"

"Yes, but Phillip isn't there."

"I'm surprised he let you out of his sight. You're too precious a gem to let slip away."

"That's something you know well," Torianna retorted.

"Ouch!" Nick made a face. Changing the subject, he asked, "How do you find life in the Poconos, now that you're back?"

"I didn't come here to talk about myself."

Nick swung around in his chair and faced his friend again. "I'm sorry."

Torianna sensed his sincerity.

"What did you come here for? Certainly not to look at dead bodies. You're way out of your jurisdiction."

"I came to see you."

That caught Nick's attention and his tone turned serious. "You came by just to see me?"

"Yes." Torianna answered quietly. Their meeting started poorly; she hoped to end well. Discussions always ended as fights with Phillip. Torianna wanted something different here...a peaceful experience.

* * *

They sat outside by the freshwater pond behind her grandmother's house, a place often frequented in their past. Torianna leaned back on the blanket and watched Nick skip rocks across the placid water. She listened as he talked, and memories of her childhood and teenage years raced through her mind. She had not often thought about such things. She wondered if Nick had.

He whirled around and walked back to the blanket. He closed his eyes, in pensive silence as he leaned against the rough tree bark. Torianna watched Nick, his silence unnerving her. She feared long silences. She wanted to speak, but no coherent thoughts formed on her lips. Nick slowly slid down onto the blanket, his shirt catching on the bark. He leaned against the strong oak, his eyes still tightly closed.

"Does it hurt to think about Lynn?" Torianna's question brought Nick's head up. She nervously munched on a slice of cheese. "I'm sorry, if I upset you," she whispered.

Nick needed to shake his melancholy. "I think I've gotten over the pain. But then other times, I know that I haven't."

"It must be hard, losing someone you love."

Nick leaned on his stomach, his face resting in his hands, and stared at her intently, "Does it hurt to think about your parents?"

Torianna wanted to weep. She saw the caring in Nick's eyes, no prying motives lay hidden in his words. "I don't really think about them."

"But now that you're here," he began.

"I don't know, maybe."

Silent, Nick waited, thinking Torianna needed to talk. "I had trouble sleeping last night," she whispered. "My grandmother knew. She saw me by the railing, and I...I saw it happening all over again." She wiped her tears. "I won't sit here and cry in front of you."

"You can cry."

"But I don't want to."

He moved close to her and pulled her back so that they both laid down and looked up at the beautiful sunset sky, a perfect finish for an imperfect day.

Nick turned to look at Torianna, not expecting her face to be so close. He leaned up on his left elbow and moved down, inches from her face. His lips gently brushed hers. If she pushed him away, he would have backed off. She welcomed him. He moved closer and kissed her more deeply. He pulled away, unsure.

She stared back at him.

"I'm sorry," he whispered.

"Don't be. I didn't stop you. I didn't want to."

Nick answered silently by pulling her into the crook of his arm and they rested together, watching their perfect sunset, a stark contrast to the uncertainty invading his heart.

Chapter Six

Agatha fussed at her desk mildly irritated with her missing oil bill. The bill folder bulged more each month. Feeling like a poor steward of her money, Agatha cringed at the notices coming in demanding payment.

Torianna chose that moment to come to her grandmother's door. She noticed her grandmother's agitated state immediately and hesitated entering the room. She knocked on the slightly ajar door and waited.

Agatha turned around and smiled weakly. "Tori, dear, you're home."

Torianna sat on her grandmother's bed. "Before you ask me anything, please tell me what's bothering you so much."

Agatha's shoulders slumped in defeat. She tried desperately to hide her troubles from her granddaughter.

Torianna placed a reassuring hand on Agatha's sagging shoulders. "What is it?"

"I didn't want to tell you."

"Please, I'm here."

"Ever since your grandfather died, my financial state has gone downhill. My bills are late. I can't always make the payments. I'm sorry."

"Sorry? For what?"

"I could lose the house, dear."

Torianna sat back on the bed, her sharp intake of breath tugged at Agatha's heart. This house held the memories of Torianna's parents, her childhood, both good and bad memories; it was the only link to her mother and father. Losing the house would be like losing her parents all over again.

Leaning forward, Torianna hugged Agatha tightly and smiled through her tears. "You are not going to lose the house, grandma. I won't let that happen."

Agatha's heart swelled with pride over her granddaughter's giving heart. Her hope reborn, she laughed through her tears, "You're wrong."

Torianna looked puzzled.

"*We* won't lose the house."

Agatha embraced her granddaughter. "Oh my goodness! I better get downstairs before I burn the house down with over baked brownies." In a flurry, they left Agatha's bedroom.

* * *

Torianna bit into the brownie, the warm chocolate melting in her mouth.

"Well, how do they taste?"

"As good as ever, of course."

"So are you going to make me wait all night to hear about you and Nick?"

Torianna took a sip of milk and smiled. "I went to the lab and then we had a picnic by the pond."

"That's it! No details," Agatha giggled like a schoolgirl conspirator.

"There's not much to tell."

"Come now."

Torianna's face grew serious and she blurted out, "Phillip doesn't deserve me."

"Now why would you say that?"

"Because I let Nick kiss me."

Agatha chuckled.

"I don't find this humorous."

"You don't know how long I've been waiting for this. Ever since you and Nick broke up years ago. I was disappointed, but I always hoped."

Torianna sat up, shocked. "There's nothing to hope for. It was just a simple kiss"

"I don't think so. If it was so harmless, then why do you feel so guilty?"

Torianna stammered, "I, uh, I don't know."

"So this is why you came here alone?"

"What do you mean?"

"You left Phillip behind because you weren't sure if you love him."

Torianna's silence said volumes.

"If things were so serious with you and Phillip, you would've brought him here to see me sooner."

"But I've been busy."

"Tori, I live two hours away from you. You've been avoiding coming here for years. I know you're busy with work, but you can't substitute that for family."

"I haven't been doing that."

Agatha replied, "Tori, you need to give up this burden soon, before you can't carry it any longer."

* * *

Torianna opened the screen door and walked out to the gazebo. Her grandmother's words demanded her attention. *You need to relax and just be; sit still and listen for His voice. You may not get any answers tonight, but that doesn't mean that He doesn't hear you. He is always listening. We are the ones who stray from His voice.*

Torianna brought her grandmother's Bible out to the gazebo with her. She left hers back in her apartment collecting dust on a bookshelf.

Leaning back in the lawn chair inside the gazebo, Torianna closed her eyes and listened to the tranquil night air. She heard the crickets chirping in the grass singing their night song in harmony with the frogs calling down in the pond. Her ears picked up the sound of a bird flying past from the tree up above and landing safely on the post of the birdhouse. She saw the bird pecking busily at the birdseed and she remembered her grandmother telling her a long time ago about Jesus caring for his children. *Worrying won't add a single hour to our lives. If He cares for the sparrow, can't He always watch over us?*

Torianna opened her heart to hear her God's voice, the still silent voice buried deep within her own heart by her own doing. She had put God in a box and only let Him out when she needed something; even then, she would rarely let Him out to work in her life.

The crickets continued to sing their night song and the bird finished his meal and flew away. The air around her grew restless, blowing through the screen. Torianna felt the breeze wash over her body, renewing her senses. She felt the Holy Spirit well up inside her, His presence a powerful force, beckoning her to fall prostrate before the Father. Overcome, Torianna asked the Lord to forgive her. She needed His cleansing power. She needed His healing for a wearied soul. She needed His protection, His guidance, and His direction for her life.

God's presence lit her spirit in a new way, foreign to her, yet welcome all the same. This is the peace she was looking for and had not been able to find. The crickets continued their song and the soft night air covered her in its warm embrace.

* * *

In bed after reading the Bible, Nick ruminated on his bizarre day. The supposed suicide of Mrs. Wilkins puzzled him. His sense of foreboding about this case rattled him. He wanted to solve the glove factor, but he knew that job belonged to forensics; not too keen on handing the glove over to that department, Nick prayed about it, and felt God leading him to keep the glove. *And do what with it? I certainly don't know how I can examine it accurately without damaging the evidence, if there is anything to prove from it ... and if the supposed evidence is still intact ...*

He huffed and sat up in bed, just wanting to forget about the glove. Not able to call Sheila since he promised not to involve her in his work after she resigned, Nick thought about his possible avenues for help.

Torianna. Her name popped in his head, along with her beautiful face. He remembered the feel of her lips on his, but then stopped. *I can't be thinking about her. There's no future there. I let her go a long time ago.*

"Maybe she'd be willing to help me," he said aloud. "She has access to a fantastic forensics lab, exactly what the doctor ordered."

Nick stood to his feet in frustration. He forced himself not to ask Torianna for help. *It would not be fair. But I want to see her again.* That realization halted his pacing. He wondered at the possibility of still caring for her after his years of marriage to Lynn.

Arresting these thoughts intruding his mind, Nick walked into the living room and stared outside into the blackness. Smoky's drooling tongue wet Nick's hand pushing his heavy thoughts into the recesses of his mind for a moment, a good moment, of welcome distraction.

Chapter Seven

An abandoned warehouse stood on the West End of town, a few miles off the interstate. Plans had been made to tear down the old building, but the demolition plans never materialized. Inside the warehouse, the damp air smelled and cobwebs covered the corners. Unopened crates collected dust on the other side of the building. New crates arrived today, which stood waiting for the warehouse doors to be opened.

* * *

"Tori, you have a visitor."

Torianna sat up from her relaxed position on the sofa. "Who is it, grandma?"

"Nick," she chirped happily, and left the room

Nick, what is he doing here? I must look a mess. Torianna smoothed her short hair in place and waited, not knowing what to expect.

Nick came in the den and gestured with his hand asking if he could join her on the sofa. Torianna nodded and waited patiently for him to talk to her.

"What is it, Nick? You look very preoccupied."

"Do I?" Nick laughed. "Well," he began carefully, "I have a big favor to ask you, but I feel bad asking it."

Torianna smiled. "Are you afraid I'll say no?"

"Maybe."

"After the nice evening you gave me last night, I'll think about doing you a favor."

Nick moved closer on the sofa, grinning. "It was nice, wasn't it?"

Torianna feigned irritation at his nearness; she playfully pushed him away. "Yes, but don't push your luck."

Serious again, Nick said, "I need the use of your forensic lab."

"*My* forensic lab? It's not mine."

"I know that, but you have access to it. I don't."

"What about your own department's lab?"

"That's just it...I don't trust them."

"Nick, what's with the cloak and dagger routine?"

Nick just smiled.

"Whatever you're talking about, it's not something to find humor in."

"I know, but I need your help."

Torianna exhaled loudly. "But I'm on vacation. I wasn't supposed to even think about work."

"Doctor Phillip's orders?"

Torianna made a face. "Don't bring him into this."

Nick paced the room. He came back and crouched down in front of Torianna's feet, placing his hands on her knees. He looked soberly into her eyes. "I wouldn't ask you if I didn't think this was serious. I don't want to bother you." Torianna looked doubtful. "It won't even seem like work. We'll stop off at the lab and then make a day of it. We'll sight-see and have another picnic."

"Since I'll be there, maybe I should stop in and see Phillip."

"He'll probably be busy," Nick remarked dryly, "but we'll make the stop."

Torianna stood up abruptly, not liking the way her heart beat faster. She said, "I'll do this only if you promise to tell me everything."

"Agreed. Shall we go, m' lady," Nick asked in all politeness, offering her his arm.

* * *

Inside the warehouse, a dark shadow flitted through the maze of crates and equipment lining the aisles. He entered through the back door, unseen, not that anyone ever came this far out of town eliminating his chances of discovery. The citizens of the town stayed away from the remote West End. Nothing of interest remained here but the old railroad tracks and shacks and the abandoned warehouse. The man carried a flashlight with him; thin streams of sunlight filtered through the cracks in the walls, but not enough for good vision.

His gloved hand ran over the wooden tops of the crates and he grinned wickedly. *What a big shipment this time.* He stopped by one of the crates near the front of the aisle and picked up the crowbar leaning against the side wall. He wedged the crowbar underneath the top of the crate and pressed down. The wooden lid opened easily for him and he removed it and the packing straw inside. He looked at the items; satisfied with what he saw, he replaced the packing straw and wooden lid. *My plan is going according to schedule.* He left the crowbar leaning against the wall and crept quietly out the warehouse, leaving through the back door.

* * *

Torianna stared out the window, watching the cars go past. Nick offered to drive to the city. It was the least he could do, he had said. *A rubber glove? All this trouble over a glove.*

"What's on your mind?"

"Oh, uh, nothing," Torianna lied.

"C'mon, tell me. You can't be sitting there and not be thinking anything."

"Since you asked," Torianna turned towards Nick, "I was thinking that you've dragged me out here on a wild goose chase."

"Tori, I'm surprised at you. I thought you would've been excited about my sleuthing."

"Not really. I've had as much as I want."

"Do you want to go back?" Nick asked, hoping she didn't.

"No, we came this far."

Nick glanced at her, wondering about her agitation. *Maybe she doesn't want to run into Phillip. Then again, maybe she does. I'm not so sure that will happen, not if I can help it.* "Are you thinking about Phillip?"

Torianna's head snapped up. "Phillip? No. Why?" She asked.

"Because he's your fiancé. He's probably thinking about you."

"Sure." She remained silent for a moment. "You know," she began more loudly than she had wanted to. "I'm getting a little tired of you and my grandmother questioning me and telling me what to think and feel about Phillip. Right now, I don't know how I feel. That was the purpose of this trip. And now I'm going back to the city after being gone for only a few days. What if I run into him, huh? Then what? And he'll see me with you. That'll take some explaining."

Nick sighed. He wanted to spend some time with Torianna, but her angry reaction surprised him. *You sure messed up again, Nick!* He spoke in a quiet voice, not wanting to upset her further. "I'm really sorry, Red, please believe me."

Torianna looked surprised by Nick's use of his pet name for her. He nicknamed her "Red" years ago. She remembered the exact spot, down at the pond by her grandmother's house; her mom had called her in to dinner...*mom, why did you leave me...* Torianna sniffled.

"Are you okay?"

"Yeah, I'm fine," she answered abruptly.

Nick inched down the highway, quickly filling up with more traffic. The silence began to make him uncomfortable. He just wanted to get to the lab and head home.

* * *

Detective Mahoney watched in surprise as Torianna walked over to his desk. His surprise increased when he saw her with another man, other than Phillip. "Hey there, Silverman, how's it going?"

"Just peachy, Mahoney. I need to speak with Janice in forensics. Have you seen her today?"

"Yeah. She's down there."

47

Torianna tapped his shoulder and started to leave. Mahoney grabbed her hand and held it protectively. "Are you okay?" he whispered.

"I'm fine," Torianna winked at him, "Thanks for asking." She glanced at Nick, "This is Nick Keyes, an old friend."

"Ahh...," Mahoney nodded knowingly, "I see."

Torianna hit him in the shoulder. "There's nothing to see." She stepped in front of Nick and moved past the desk.

"You'd better hurry after her. You could get lost," Mahoney motioned to Nick to follow Detective Silverman.

Doubling his stride to catch up with Torianna, Nick asked, "What was that all about?"

"Nothing. Mahoney's a joker."

"Oh." Nick followed Torianna's determined stride not understanding where her annoyance came from. She could be in such a volatile mood and then purr like a contented cat. *This job must be getting to her.*

Inside the forensics lab, Torianna introduced Nick to her friend and fellow officer, Janice Kennig. Janice ushered them over to the counter where she tested blood samples. She asked them to wait for a moment. Nick's eyes roamed around the lab; he was lost in thought when Torianna elbowed him in the ribs as Janice asked to see his evidence bag.

"Oh, excuse me, I was just admiring your facility."

"Thank you," Janice replied. "Let's take a look."

Janice brought the bag over to a different counter, one cleared of equipment, and opened the bag. Her gloved hand carefully removed the rubber glove. She examined it closely and made a mental note of something she saw before placing the glove back in the bag. "How long have you had this glove?"

"Since about three or four o'clock yesterday morning. Why? Did I do something wrong?"

"No, as a matter of fact, you did something right. When Tori phoned me that you had a blood sample on a rubber glove, I was hoping that you hadn't stored it in a plastic bag. Down in the lab, we can easily work with dried blood, but not with rotted blood. The plastic would've kept it airtight."

Nick breathed a sigh of relief. He had worried about possibly damaging the blood sample.

Beside him, Torianna examined the rubber glove, an inquiring look forming on her face.

"What do you see?" Janice asked.

"Could the perp possibly have left prints behind through the glove? The material appears thin enough."

"If we're lucky, and the perp had pronounced ridges on his hands, then we can pick something up. What about the weapon?"

Torianna regarded Nick and he answered sheepishly, "I don't know. My department has it with the other evidence."

Janice nodded understandingly. "They don't know you have this glove."

Nick rose to his defense. "They didn't see it and I knew they weren't going to pick it up. You see, our Ident team is not very good. Actually, we have only part-timers," he answered lamely.

"Janice, Nick here thinks that someone in his department is covering up a scandal. He's into this cloak and dagger stuff. His favorite author is Agatha Christie."

"Oh." Janice smiled and resealed the glove in the bag. "So what do you expect to find from this sample?" She directed her question at her colleague.

"Can you do a DNA sampling of the blood and check for any latent prints?"

Janice looked surprised. "You're the fingerprint expert, Tori, why don't you do them?"

"She's supposed to be on vacation," Nick cut in.

"Okay," Janice laughed, knowing that her friend had a hard time relaxing. This little escapade proved it. Janice also suspected that this drive down to the lab was not Tori's idea.

"I'll call you with the results. Are you at Agatha's house?"

"Yeah. We'll be waiting for your call." Torianna thanked her friend and she left the lab with Nick.

Chapter Eight

As soon as they left the building, Nick reached for Torianna's hand. He led her down the stairs and across the street. He spied a hot dog stand on the corner. Torianna went along with him, thankful for his decision to get something to eat. Nick asked for ketchup and relish on Tori's hotdog and mustard on his. Torianna smiled that he remembered what she liked on her hotdog. Nick asked Torianna to hold the hotdogs while he took some bills out of his wallet.

They walked along the sidewalk and came to a park bench a bit further down. Torianna enjoyed the quiet conversation with Nick after they'd finished their *Sabrettes*. They sat facing one another on the bench, laughing and reminiscing. Nick explained to Torianna how the town elected him as county coroner, which delighted him at first. Then, when he realized all the work involved, he felt inadequate to the challenging tasks.

Torianna grinned and wondered how he managed without his able assistant. Rewarded with a bright toothy grin, Nick explained his first autopsy without Sheila at his side. Not expecting all the details when he first started to explain, Torianna almost told Nick to stop before her lunch revisited her mouth.

Nick reminded Torianna of his reaction when he first saw her again in the lab. Torianna laughed and put her hand lightly on his arm, which rested on the top of the bench. A shadow passed over her seated form at just that moment. Torianna's heart stopped at the voice coming to her ears.

"Tori! What are you doing here?"

Torianna gasped; she looked guiltily up at her fiancé. "Phillip," she said with a bit more calm than she felt. Torianna refused to look over at Nick when she felt his gaze on her.

Phillip stared at Torianna, his face unhappy. He waited for his fiancée to answer his question.

"I was just talking."

"I can see that. But you're not supposed to be in New York. I believe you're on vacation."

"I am on vacation."

"I must be misunderstanding something here," Phillip began.

Nick tried to come to Torianna's aid, "You see, I'm the one who asked Tori to come here with me."

Phillip glared at Nick, but directed his question towards Torianna. "Who is he?"

Nick stifled his laughter. *Who is this guy? C'mon, Red, you could've done better than this.*

Torianna smiled at Nick and tried to keep her cool. "This is Nick Keyes. He's an old friend of mine."

"Renewing an old acquaintance, I see."

Torianna shivered slightly under Phillip's hard stare. His display of anger startled Torianna.

"I thought you wanted to be alone?" Phillip interrogated.

"I did — do — want to be alone."

"Than what's he doing here with you? You two seem quite cozy."

Nick tried to speak up again in Torianna's defense. "No, really, we came here because I needed to get something to the lab. Tori's department is much more advanced than mine."

Phillip doubted Nick's sincerity. He looked at Torianna again. "You could've told me you were coming back."

"But I'm not coming back, not now. My vacation's not over yet."

"Yeah, I know, " Phillip retorted. "I'm not sure what to think. You've been distant for the past few months. I can't talk to you anymore. You won't let me."

"That's not true," Torianna argued, but she knew he was right.

Phillip waved his hand at Nick, "You can talk to him. I'm not good enough for you?"

Torianna remained silent.

"If that's how you want it..." Phillips words hung in the air.

"What are you talking about?"

"You're free now. I'll get out of your life." Phillip whirled away.

Torianna felt exhausted. She glanced at Nick and he laid his hand on hers. "C'mon, let's head home."

Torianna stood up and pulled him back. "Wait. I want to go to my apartment."

Nick looked puzzled.

"We're here, and I like to take a hot shower right now."

* * *

The hot water ran down Torianna's head, drenching her head and streaming down her back. Her tears mingled with the hot water on her face. Phillip's disappointment intruded her thoughts; his pained face, as he walked away, haunted her mind. She closed her eyes, trying to wash the memory away. The steam fogged up the small bathroom. She turned her water off and grabbed her towel. She rubbed her face with the towel and then heard Nick knock on the door.

"One second," Torianna called. She wrapped the towel around her and put on her robe, then opened the door a crack. He handed her a cup of cinnamon tea. She smiled her thanks and put the cup on the counter.

Nick touched her face and whispered, "Everything's gonna be all right." He looked down at her hand and saw the diamond still in place.

Torianna followed his gaze. "Oh. I guess I don't need this anymore. Here." She took it off; she had to tug a little at first. "You take it."

Nick laughed, "What am I gonna do with it?"

"I don't care," Torianna turned around.

"Do you have Phillip's address somewhere? To mail it back to him," Nick answered her confused look.

"Check in my desk. In one of the right drawers. I have envelops with his address."

Nick squeezed her hand and left the bathroom, closing the door behind him. Torianna looked down at her left hand, the ring finger bare, but she still felt the engagement ring embracing her finger.

Nick found the envelop with Phillip's address and he got the engagement ring settled in a package and out of the way before Torianna emerged from the bathroom. She moved over to Nick and asked if he wanted something to drink.

She carried two sodas to the table and joined Nick on the sofa. His arm shifted companionably around her and pulled Torianna against his chest. Her head rested on his shoulder. He leaned his strong chin on her head, squeezed her in a reassuring hug, and whispered that everything would be fine. *I'm not going to lose her this time. My Red is back and I won't let her go.*

Relishing their intimacy, Torianna cried herself to sleep in Nick's arms. Nick reflected upon the events of the past few days. To some, their romance might seem to be progressing rapidly, but Nick knew differently. Having a friendship that spanned years and a passionate season, Nick gladly accepted a return to their love.

* * *

Back in the car, Torianna slept while Nick drove to the Poconos. He watched the road and concentrated on what lay ahead. Nick promised himself to give Torianna breathing room in their relationship. Certain of his affections, he wanted to wait until she made the next move.

He excitedly thought about Janice's tests. He hoped for a blood sample intact enough to yield good results. If they discovered prints on the glove...then the chance at discovering who...*who, what?* Nick interrupted his own rambling thoughts. *What am I trying to prove, anyway? Yeah, I found the glove, but that doesn't mean it has any relation to the murder, well, "suicide." I know this isn't so cut and dry. I've got to find out. And Red, you've got to believe me. I trust my gut feeling.* Nick abandoned his thoughts. Torianna stirred and he wanted to listen if she needed to talk. *I feel like taking you home with me and never letting you go back to the city and your life there, Red.*

Chapter Nine

Sitting at his desk, Detective Mitchell Daniels thought about his current investigation. *Sherry Wilkins.* Certain aspects of this case bothered him. He knew the coroner who handled the autopsy. *Keyes. But what were you thinking, Nick? What was he supposed to do, I guess. It was an apparent suicide. It just doesn't seem to match up.*

Chief Roberts had instructed Mitchell to keep a lid on a possible scandal. The town heard reports of the suicide on the news, an inevitable occurrence. However, the Chief told Mitchell that if he went poking his nose around disputing the coroner's opinion, that he must use discretion.

Mitchell shrugged and leaned back in his chair. "It's no use, Lord," he whispered, "I've tried to find the truth in this case. Maybe the autopsy was right and it was suicide. But I knew Sherry. She never would have killed herself." Mitchell closed his eyes and smiled at the sweet memory which haunted his mind ever since he viewed Sherry's body, her beautiful body in a heap on the floor.

A younger Mitchell ran through the woods, chasing after the tall thin form running ahead. He saw her blond hair swaying in the wind and he wanted to reach out and touch the softness, feel her body in his arms and hear her whisper his name. He ran faster, jumping over rocks, jutting branches and bushes. Sherry turned around and smiled, not noticing the danger in front of her. Mitchell called out her name, in warning. She ignored his words of caution, thinking he teased her.

She tripped over a root and landed on her hands and knees. Mitchell caught up with her and cradled her in his arms. She laughed and said she was all right, especially since his strong arms wrapped protectively around her. She smiled up at him, eagerly accepting his warm kisses.

The sound of the phone ringing brought Mitchell to the present. *"Why, Sherry, why didn't you listen to me? Why did you marry him?"* He expertly hid his anguish and answered his phone.

* * *

Garbed in a faded dress, Agatha knelt by her garden pulling weeds; her wide-brimmed straw hat shaded her eyes from the sunlight. Her gardening gloves protected her hands against calluses from handling the shovel and spade so much. Agatha peeked up from under the rim of her straw hat and saw Torianna farther down in the garden.

Her heart ached for her granddaughter. Nick had spoken with Agatha last night after he and Torianna got home and Torianna settled in bed. Nick told Agatha all the details including his feelings for Torianna. Of course, Agatha found great joy in that fact; she longed to take Torianna's hurt away. But Agatha felt peace since Torianna rested here under the protection of the Lord and her watchful eye. Agatha took comfort knowing that Nick remained constantly at Torianna's side.

The pleasant sound of the birds chirping filled the backyard. Agatha and Torianna felt hope in the sounds of the nature surrounding them. The sun was not extremely bright today and Agatha was grateful for that. It made for easier gardening weather.

Nick had promised Agatha not to rush Torianna into a relationship. Agatha nodded approvingly. She trusted the young man completely with her granddaughter. At the moment, Nick was working hard on one particular case file and he made Agatha promise to keep Torianna calm and rested while he was gone. Nick told Torianna that he would ask for her help only if he desperately needed it. He said she should act like she really was on vacation. And that she did. Torianna had been resting nicely for the past few days. She almost was sad that she would be leaving after next week.

* * *

"Detective Daniels here."

"Hey, Mitchell. It's me, Nick."

Mitchell sat forward in his chair. "What?"

"You can start by being a bit more civil to your friend."

Mitchell rubbed his head. "I'm sorry, Nick. I've been tense lately."

"I can understand," Nick knew the history between Mitchell and Sherry Wilkins.

"What's up?" Mitchell tried sounding cheerful.

"I need to meet with you."

Mitchell laughed. "What is this? Some kind of rendezvous?"

"Kind of."

"Really?"

"I have some important information that I'd like to share with you. You may find it extremely interesting."

Mitchell dared to hope. "Information about what?"

"A certain case file I've been working on."

"I see. I can meet you later today."

"At the park."

"See ya then."

* * *

Torianna strolled through her grandmother's yard, an acre of property which extended into a wooded area beyond the house. She passed by the pond behind the back porch. Picking up a flat rock, Torianna skipped it across the placid water. Her thoughts turned to the evening she shared with Nick out here by the pond, the first time he kissed her in many years. *Too many, actually.* She grabbed a thin stick from the ground and began breaking apart pieces of the dead twig and throwing it into the water as she walked along the edge of the pond. Her mind traveled to the other night when she renewed her commitment before the Lord.

It felt good in her spirit, right, somehow to belong to the Lord and let Him rule her life, to give her guidance and support…give her peace…to be her protector. With one week left of her vacation, Torianna began to dread going back to the city, not such a beautiful place as her childhood home. Here the grass was so green and the trees swayed in the wind on cool summer nights.

Torianna felt bad for leading Phillip on. Guiltily, she wondered why she had accepted his engagement. Maybe the romantic atmosphere clouded her focus. The snow falling made for a magical moment, the night Phillip proposed. Perhaps she said yes, hoping it would always be a fairy tale. Torianna now realized she loved Phillip as a friend, his kindness and thoughtfulness the attraction.

Torianna's steps grew heavier as she continued walking into deeper paths, towards the forest. Her eyes took in the wonders of the forest in the late afternoon. The green leaves blanketed her small form in a comforting canopy, *like God's love,* she thought. Her footsteps carried her over the rocky incline until she came to a flat boulder above the pond, an overlook.

She saw the water bubble with tiny air pockets from the fish swimming close to the surface. She heard a bullfrog's mating call; he sat on a lily pad, mouth opening wide.

The air carried a soft breeze and Torianna welcomed it, like a cooling balm. She closed her eyes and bowed in reverence for her Father's creation. She knew with a certainty that He would guide her and she asked for cleansing from the pain she caused Phillip. She prayed for Phillip, for the Lord's protection. Sitting on the rock in silence, Torianna rested in the Lord's presence. She had an assurance overwhelm her and she knew that somehow everything would turn out fine. She had a sense of new adventure and was open to God leading her.

* * *

Nick waited on the park bench for his fellow officer. He noticed Mitchell walking towards him, his face skeptical. Nick rose to his feet and they shook hands.

"So, Nick, why'd we have to meet in private?"

"I think you should sit down."

"Really? This better be good."

"Oh, it's good all right."

"Well, then get too it, man."

Nick leaned forward on the bench, his body motions excited as he spoke. Instinct told him to tread carefully on this subject, in the face of his friend's fresh grief. "When I first did the autopsy, I knew what everyone seemed to expect from me, especially the chief. I had a feeling it was not a suicide, but all the evidence pointed to that."

"So why'd you call it a suicide?"

"Look, all the examinations pointed towards a suicide. But there was something I found that made me suspicious."

Now Mitchell leaned forward. "What did you find?"

"I found a rubber glove out on the side of the house on the way to my car."

"What's so special about that?"

"I wasn't sure at the time. But my gut told me it was important. Now I'm glad I picked it up."

"Did anyone ever tell you that you take too long telling a story?"

"But this is a good tale, my friend. Anyway, the glove had a blood stain on the index finger and there appeared to be metal tracings from a gun."

"That means," Mitchell began, a smile creeping up on his face.

Nick held up a hand, "Let's not jump the gun. It means that Sherry's blood was found on the glove. So, either she killed herself with the gloves on and then somehow they got off, or someone wanted to make it look like a suicide and was wearing the gloves at the time of the shooting."

"I prefer the latter. May I ask how you got away with this?"

"I had access to the forensics lab in the NYPD."

"Whew!" Mitchell looked surprised. "What was your access code?" He laughed.

"Red. She's back."

"Torianna Silverman. Wow! You work fast."

"It's not like that," Nick argued.

"Maybe you can try to keep her this time," Mitchell joked.

"Funny. Everyone seems to be making fun at my expense lately."

Chapter Ten

Jonas rested on the sofa across from Agatha in her living room; they both enjoyed hot cinnamon tea. The evening still young, Agatha sighed contentedly, thankful for her long, relaxing day. She had worked some more in her garden, tending to the pesky weeds which seemed to poke up quicker each time she pulled others out. She was beginning to think the weeds had a conspiracy against her and her garden.

Jonas interrupted her thoughts to speak to Agatha about the talk he heard around town today. *For a man,* Agatha thought, *he sure does a lot of gossiping.* She knew the harm in gossip running wild, but when Jonas started talking, you never could stop him. Agatha thought of him as a little wind up toy that just kept spinning, never reaching the point of stillness.

Relaxing across from her companion, Agatha silently admitted to not paying much attention to his ramblings. Not considering herself rude, she simply watched him, observing his antics. She noticed that he looked fairly fatigued lately, and not just a weariness brought on by pranks of the neighborhood boys. He had a weariness that went deep. She began to uplift him in prayer to the Father.

Agatha smiled and nodded in the appropriate places, until her head sprang up in attention, not sure if she heard correctly. *What was that about the Mayor's wife?* Agatha moved to the edge of her chair, ears alert, wanting Jonas to continue talking. This news disturbed Agatha.

"There's talk around town that the Mayor's wife, poor thing, didn't commit suicide. They say she was murdered." Jonas knew he had an audience now and he delightedly continued. "I don't know what to think. Why, the police already said it was suicide. Why would they lie, huh? Maybe the police were wrong. Oh, my goodness, Aggie," he looked anxious, "that means we have a murderer on our hands."

Agatha grew worried then, not because of Jonas' alarm, but because rumors like this had harmful potential to the town. "Jonas, I don't know who told you this, but it's not true. Nobody killed dear Sherry. It was a sad state she was in. You know what the police said. It's a shame, but it's the truth."

Jonas stood up and began pacing the room. He appeared even more agitated than normal; Agatha worried about him. "Can you be sure, Aggie? They could have been lying to us, to the whole town."

"Now why would they do that, Jonas? The police are here to protect us. I know Chief Roberts, and I know Nick. Nick did the autopsy and I'm sure he did a fine job."

Not placated by Agatha's words, Jonas shook his head and continued pacing the room. "My insides don't lie and I'm shaking in my boots."

Fed up with this nonsense, Agatha marched over to Jonas and turned him around. "Now you listen here, Jonas Martin. There is no murderer in this town. You know that and I know that. We both have rational minds. We have to think like rational people. Look at me, Jonas," she shook him slightly, "don't you know that God is here protecting us? Come, now, dear. Let's finish our tea." She guided him to the sofa and handed him his cup of tea. "Drink this, then I'll get us some fresh tea if you'd like."

Jonas obediently sipped his tea and kept his mouth shut. His eyes focused on something Agatha could not see. Frustrated with his behavior, she just let him sit still for a moment. Agatha tried to shrug off the disturbing gossip, but deep in the pit of her stomach, she knew that her friend was not going insane. *He may be eccentric, but he's still very sane. This thing has gotten him extremely shaken up. Maybe there's something to it. Oh, stop being so foolish, she chided herself, there's nothing to the town gossip.*

* * *

Agatha relaxed in her bedroom, reading. A few hours had passed since Jonas calmed down enough for her to agree to let him walk home. Still early, she decided to relax in her room with a good book. She read through three chapters when Jonas' distressing words kept coming back to her head. Not wanting to dwell on the bad thoughts, she tried to clear her mind, but the thoughts troubled her. Agatha sat back in the chair and put her book on the window ledge.

She had brought another cup of tea with her, decaffeinated, of course; she needed to sleep at night. But the tea failed to calm her. She needed something else, something more reliable. She chuckled at her lack of faith, which the Lord so gently revealed to her. Here she fretted over something quite imaginary, when she had the Lord, a being so real in her life, to whom she could turn. She smiled and walked over to her bed; reaching for her Bible, she settled in for a long session with the Lord.

Agatha's hands searched for her beloved Psalm 91. As her eyes focused on the words, she read His promise. *For He will command His angels concerning you to guard you in all your ways; they will lift you up in their hands, so that you will not strike your foot against a stone.* She trusted His promise, a promise made especially for a time like this.

She believed in angels. She knew that God sent them to His people as ministering spirits, helping His servants. She wanted to be God's servant, to do whatever He would have her do. She knew God sent Torianna to her home in this time of need. Agatha would be there for her. She also knew that God purposed something else for her to do — pray for her family, for Nick, and for the town of paradise... for the restoration of the glory of the Lord. She vowed to look to the Father of Light and watch for His glory to descend and shine about her.

Agatha moved off the chair to her knees. Prostrate before the Lord, she spoke of her love for Him and His creation. She spoke praises to His name. *Holy Father. Emmanuel. Almighty. God with us. Alpha and Omega.* She repeated His name over and over, basking in

His presence. Agatha whispered words of endearment. She asked forgiveness for sins which she neglected to speak to the Lord about. She asked for guidance for her and the money she needed to keep the house. She hated the thought of Torianna being burdened with her grandmother's problems. Agatha sought direction for Tori and peace for her heart. She thanked the Lord for bringing Tori to her knees in recommitment to Christ. Agatha prayed for her town, for peace to once again be restored to the quiet place she called home.

Chapter Eleven

Outside, Torianna and Nick sat in the gazebo. "Your grandmother must think me rude for keeping you out here to myself," Nick teased.

"Nonsense, she's inside with Jonas, no doubt getting a headache from his incessant talking. I bet right now, grandma is watching him, but trying to tune him out."

"You're probably right. You know her better than I do, so I won't wager a guess."

"No, I'm sure of it. I'll even prove it to you."

"What?" Nick asked as Torianna dragged him out of the gazebo. *She's in rare form tonight. So happy, and at peace. And ready to leave in a few days. I'm not looking forward to that. I've got to do something to get her to stay. Asking her to marry me is out of the question, at least for a while. She'd never accept now. But what can I do?* Nick pondered ideas in his head, finding nothing workable. *There has to be something. That's it,* he almost shouted, but caught himself in time. Torianna shook Nick's arm. "What's the matter? You haven't been listening to me. Don't tell me you were tuning me out. I didn't think I was that boring."

If you only knew, Red. "I was, uh, just thinking about work."

"Thanks. That's encouraging. I guess you do find me boring."

Way to go. Try again, he chided himself.

"No, I wasn't really thinking about work. I was...oh, never mind. Now, please refresh my memory. I'd forgotten the stimulating conversation we were having."

Torianna smiled sweetly and pulled him towards the hallway, but motioned for him to stay quiet. She walked to the side of the livingroom behind her grandmother so she remained out of sight. Torianna knew Jonas would be so engrossed in his monologue that he wouldn't see them standing in the hallway. Nick tried to figure out why Torianna told him to stand in the hallway. Not minding, Nick willingly watched Torianna without her seeing him. She motioned him closer and made him peek in the room. She was correct. Agatha watched Jonas and nodded at the correct places. Nick smiled, glad he made no wager.

On their way back out to the gazebo, they stopped in the kitchen for one of Agatha's ever present treats. With two younger people always in and out of her house now, she promised to fatten them up. Nick and Torianna walked back to the gazebo and noticed the setting sun and the darkness about to envelop them. Torianna flipped the switch and lights went on in the gazebo.

"Wow, I didn't know you had lights here."

"Yeah. My grandfather put them in when he built the gazebo." She grew quiet, "My parents loved to sit out here and talk. I remember that I used to play right there on the floor with my dolls. I didn't realize how much I missed my parents until I came home." Nick's heart saddened at Torianna's admission. In an effort not to dampen the evening, Torianna tried to talk about something else. "How is work going?"

He stretched his arms over his head and yawned, "It's going great, but very tiring."

"Too bad you don't have an assistant anymore."

Maybe now's my chance. Nick cleared his throat nervously and leaned forward. "Do you like it here?"

"Here? You mean, Hilltop?"

"Yeah. Well, do you?" prompted Nick.

"Of course I do. I have bad memories here, but also lots of good ones."

Her response encouraged Nick. "Is that why you left for New York?" Nick asked.

Torianna spoke in an unnaturally open fashion with him tonight.

"I left for New York because we broke up."

Those words hit Nick hard, like a blow to the chest. He didn't know how to respond at first. *All this time and I never knew. Now what do I say?*

"Are you surprised?" Torianna asked.

Nick leaned back against the chair. "Yeah. I had no idea."

"Maybe you were too caught up in the circumstances."

"Perhaps." His well-laid plan began to go awry. He had no desire to rehash the past. He cared about Torianna too much for that. "Let's not get into the past. It's history. And this is a new beginning for us."

She stared at him, not wanting to hope. "Can it be that easy for us?"

"Do you like New York, living in the city?"

"Why all these questions?" She asked.

Nick moved closer, his elbows resting on his knees, his full attention on her. "Please just answer the question. I need to know."

"Okay," she responded, resting in her chair, pulling her knees up to her chin. "I don't know, really. I never thought about it much. I was just there. I guess I adapted to the city; I got used to it."

"So that means you could move, without any regrets."

Silence met Nick, and his confidence wavered, but he kept firm in his resolve to finish explaining his plan.

"Well," she started, "I guess." She looked down at her hands, resting on her feet. "I don't have Phillip anymore. So there's really no attachment there. But," she sought his eyes, "I love my job. That's the one thing I would miss if I left." She put her feet down, shifted her body forward, her face close to Nick's across from her. "What are we talking about?"

Anticipation in his eyes, Nick said, "About us."

"Us? That has a familiar ring to it."

"It has a good ring to it. I like it."

"You do?"

"Yes." Hesitantly Nick advanced, as if playing a game of checkers. He made a move, thinking it was a good one. Then his opponent countered his move, possibly dashing his hopes of winning. He did not want Torianna to counter attack. He wanted her to stop playing and accept his move. "Please stay in Hilltop with me."

Torianna grew still and examined Nick, searching for security in his eyes.

"You could do that, you know," Nick prodded.

"I know."

"Then what's the problem?"

"Impatient, are we?"

"Yes."

"I don't care," she teased.

"I know you do."

"Really?"

"I can see it in your eyes."

"Well, I can see it in your eyes."

"So it's settled?"

"Nope."

"Why not?"

"Where would I work?"

"I'll appoint you my deputy coroner."

"But I'm an Ident officer, not a pathologist," her hand moved to cover his, "and I'm a fingerprint specialist. Would you like me to check your prints?"

"Now?"

"Sure."

She picked up his hand and pretended to examine it. She kissed each finger, one by one. "You still haven't said yes."

"You haven't asked yet."

"I did."

"No, you said you'd appoint me as your deputy. You didn't ask. I don't like to be told. I like to be asked."

"Okay. Will you be my deputy coroner?"

"Why'd you wait so long to ask?"

"I guess that means yes?"

"No, this means yes." She put her arms around his neck and kissed his nose. Her beautiful smile lit her face.

I think that plan went well, Nick thought as he grinned contentedly.

* * *

When Torianna finally said good night to Nick and went up to her room, her grandmother was already in her own room, the door closed. Torianna heard Agatha speaking and thinking she was praying, went down the hall so as not to disturb her. Her senses whirling from all that transpired this evening, Torianna laughed and started readying herself for bed. *I can't believe I grabbed him like that. He must think I'm an animal. But he seemed to like it.*

She turned back her covers and got into bed. She read from her Bible, but hoped God excused her unfocused brain. She turned out the light and rested her head on her pillow, her new boss the last waking memory.

* * *

Nick opened the door and Smoky met him in the hallway. He bent down and rubbed his dog's ears. "Hey, boy. I've got great news. I think she really cares about me." He jumped up and did a little dance step down the hall towards the kitchen. Smoky regarded his master with an almost human look of perplexity.

Smoky followed his master into the kitchen, hoping for a bowl of food. Nick put out some food for his sheepdog and grabbed a cold drink and headed towards the living room. Too happy to sleep, he settled onto the sofa and turned on the television. He watched the late show, but a certain red head kept stealing his attention.

Chapter Twelve

An oracle is within my heart concerning the sinfulness of the wicked: there is no fear of God before his own eyes. For in his own eyes he flatters himself too much to detect or hate his sin. The words of his mouth are wicked and deceitful; he has ceased to be wise and to do good. Even on his bed he plots evil; he commits himself to a sinful course and does not reject what is wrong. Agatha read from her devotions this morning. The words of this Psalm spoke to her heart; she pitied any poor soul who rejected the Lord's way, not turning in reverence to him.

* * *

The man sat at his desk, grinning wickedly. He had heard rumors around town. People branded him a murderer. A wicked man. Of course, they extended pleasantries and absolute politeness to him in public, but in the quiet of their homes, he knew they talked about him. He ignored their gossip, not expecting any harm to come to him.

The police closed their investigation, freeing him of any guilt. His wife had committed suicide, plain and simple. He had no part in it. He came home that morning and found his poor wife, lying on the floor, blood oozing from the wound in her head. He told the police, in all innocence, that he spent the evening with his friend, not at home when the awful accident happened. He called it an accident because he said he should have paid more attention to his poor wife. *So frail,* he said. *Frail and weak. Her mind had been wavering on the point of insanity lately.* They checked out his alibi. The police believed it all.

He reached into his open drawer and pulled out the disc she made. His good sense told him to destroy it, but his vanity overcame him. He flattered himself that he got away with the perfect crime. He kept the disc. *A reminder of what could have been, dear Sherry, if only you had listened to me and went along with my plan. But you got in the way. And now your memory is tainted with insanity. And that's how I'll keep it.*

He sat, thoughts of the maid invading his mind. The night of the murder, he told her to take time off and not come back until noon. He wanted to eliminate the chance of her catching him in the act or seeing the police cars swarming his house. And it worked. *That maid, the silly little thing was grateful to get out of the house and have some time off.*

A sudden fear gripped him, but he shook it off. *It's impossible for her to know anything. She's just as stupid as Sherry. There's no way.* He abruptly stood up from his chair. He walked to the window and spied the maid beating the rugs outside, dust clouding around her. He grinned as he watched her. *She would be something. And I'm here all alone, far from any prying eyes. Maybe she'd be of more use to me than Sherry. And if I'm not pleased with her, well, then I'll let her go.*

* * *

Cindy worked hard beating the rugs by the back door. She longed to escape this house; it was trouble since the day she started. If only she had heeded her friend's advice. He had warned her, but she had desperately wanted to leave home. Her father came home drunk every night and beat her mother…she remembered her mother's tired eyes and battered face.

Cindy knew Mrs. Wilkins for 13 months and never in that time did Cindy notice her employer losing her mind. When Cindy came back to the house and heard about Mrs. Wilkins' suicide, she grew suspicious. *I'm surprised she didn't kill herself with that jerk for a husband.* Cindy quickly looked around, afraid, as if someone heard her thoughts.

A kind and gracious woman, Mrs. Wilkins used to help Cindy with the housework, much to Mr. Wilkins' dislike. He always gave her more work whenever he was home which was not as often as Cindy thought he should be. *But it's none of my business.* She felt so sorry for Mrs. Wilkins. Both women close in age, Cindy had almost wished for friendship, but the employer and employee relationship restricted them.

Cindy beat the rug against the stone steps, with a frustration that frightened her. *I know he did this to her. She wouldn't have killed herself. But what am I supposed to do about it? Who's gonna believe me? Even if I did have proof, which I don't.*

Cindy turned away from her task and scanned the vast backyard, a beautiful place marred by Sherry's brutal death. *He doesn't belong in a house like this. He's probably doing something illegal. I don't know how he keeps up this lifestyle; being Mayor here, in this small town won't get you far.*

* * *

The late afternoon sun filtered through the curtains in Darren Wilkins' office. He hung up the phone and began to pace the room, then stopped and leaned up against the front of his desk. His plan was continuing smoothly along its course. His confidence rose. And when this type of wicked confidence reached and all time high, a false sense of power affected Darren, blinding him to his true powerless position. He owned the town and remained on top of his side dealings, raking in the money; but he thought himself incapable of capture and punishment. *And I have this pretty little toy that's been right under my nose the whole time. I should have taken her before Sherry met her untimely demise. It's not as if my dear devoted wife was fulfilling her wifely duties.*

Darren walked to his window and opened it. He needed some air. He could not decide if he should ring for the little creature to come to him or if he should come after her.

* * *

Bending over in the kitchen, Cindy wiped up the puddle of milk. On edge this entire week, she feared living in this house. Darren slipped quietly into the kitchen, like a wraith in the night. He came up behind her. Her body tensed. She had been dreading this moment for a long time. Afraid to fight her employer, she remained paralyzed with fear. Cindy envisioned Mr. Wilkins firing her, leaving her nowhere to go until she found another job. And that could take weeks. She feared for her life, knowing his awful secret.

He grabbed her arms and she tried to stand up. He pulled her back against him and wrapped his arms around her upper body. She stiffened and he spoke into her ear, "Relax, this won't hurt. You'll enjoy it."

She tried to struggle out of his arms, but he drew her closer, nauseating her. His hands ran down her arms. She squirmed as he leaned forward and tried to kiss her. His breath on her neck repulsed her, and she twisted around. She broke away from his roving hands, but then his arms ensnared her, bringing them face to face. His evil stare overwhelmed her with fear. *Someone help me.*

He pulled her close and moved in, claiming her mouth intrusively; then he pushed her away, a leering smile mocking her. "Wasn't that good? It was for me."

He loosened her from his grasp and she stumbled back against the counter. She brushed her hair away from her face and whispered, tears threatening to spill. "No, I didn't like it." *I can't let him see me cry. He'll know I'm scared. Then there will be no hope of getting out of here.*

He came forward and touched her cheek. She pushed him away. "You'd better get to like it, honey, because I want you and I always get what I want," he boasted and left her standing alone in the kitchen.

She held back her tears until she got to her room in the rear of the house. She hurried inside and bolted the door. The dam of her emotions broke, crumbling any facade of control. She sat huddled on her bed, clutching a pillow, a similar pose struck in her childhood during one of her father's drunken rages; Cindy tried to forget.

* * *

A few hours later, a composed Cindy stood staring out Sherry's bedroom window. She remembered the hard lessons learned from her father, lessons instilling fear and teaching her not to cry. Today's tears shocked her; much time had passed since she wept so fiercely. But she excused her weakness because of the shock of losing her esteemed employer, and because that beast touched her.

She vowed not to cry anymore. Her fighting spirit rose to the forefront. She racked her brain for a plan to prove her employer murdered his wife. She desperately wanted to leave this house. After that incident in the kitchen, she decided to sleep out on the street if necessary. As soon as possible, Cindy wanted to leave, but an escape seemed impossible. She recalled his harsh words. *I want you and I always get what I want.*

Cindy stood inside her deceased employer's closet and finished packing her garments. Mr. Wilkins expressed his desire for Cindy to start packing the day after his wife passed away. Cindy obeyed in silent protest, resenting his callous attitude.

Near the end of the large walk-in closet, Cindy rubbed the smooth fabric of the last hanging silk dress between her fingers. She affectionately envied her employer's clothes. Mr. Wilkins had dressed his wife properly, the perfect ideal for a Mayor's wife. She never disgraced him in public. Cindy respected Mrs. Wilkins for that; she was a good woman. Cindy took down the dark winter coat that hung on the bar. She opened the plastic bag, but before she put the coat in, she checked all the pockets to see if Mrs. Wilkins left anything inside. Cindy found nothing in the other coats so this time, when her fingers touched a thin, square object, her eyebrows raised in surprise.

She pulled a disc out of the pocket. *What is this, Mrs. Wilkins? You can rest assured that I won't hand this over to Mr. Wilkins.* Cindy slipped the disc into her apron pocket. The move was very timely because the Mayor chose that moment to enter the room. Cindy let out a quick breath. *That was too close.*

He opened the dresser drawers. "I see you haven't finished with her lingerie yet?"

Cindy straightened her skirt and apron. "No sir, I haven't had the time. But I just finished with the closet."

He reached in the drawer and held up a white satin negligee, short and so silky. Cindy had often touched the silk when she washed them, but with respect for her employer and admiration of her fine clothes, not the way he touched them now. He came closer and tossed the garment on the bed. He closed the gap between them and spoke in harsh tones. "You will wear that," pointing to the silk, "when I come back. And we'll have a fun time." *He was going somewhere.* "I have some business to attend to for a few days." He got up from the bed as quickly as he had sat down, and walked out of the bedroom, closing the door. For a moment, Cindy feared he would lock the door.

Going away for a few days. Now's my chance. She stood up shakily and smoothed her clothes, feeling for the disc. She finished her cleaning and left the master bedroom. *I'm sorry Mrs. Wilkins, that I can't keep watch over your house. But I hope this will make up for it.* She quietly hurried to her room and began to pack.

Chapter Thirteen

Cindy hefted her two suitcases and duffel bag and left through the back door. Owning meager possessions when she began to work for Mr. and Mrs. Wilkins, she left with what she came, except for a small cameo broach which Mrs. Wilkins gave her last Christmas, a gift Cindy wanted to cherish forever.

She expected a grueling mile walk to the road with her luggage. She waited until morning to leave, shortly after Mr. Wilkins departed for this trip. He stayed away from her the whole night, a welcome relief for Cindy.

She called for a taxi after Mr. Wilkins left and then she started the trek down the long driveway. She wanted to eliminate any chances of Mr. Wilkins driving up to the house when she left, so she decided to meet the taxi on the road. It took her a few minutes to walk the length of the driveway. She approached the road, thankful for the absence of the taxi, not wanting to be seen walking from the house.

Although unsure where to stay until she found a new job, Cindy knew she had to get out of that house. Her life depended on it. *Mr. Wilkins is a wicked man. She was such a kind, pretty woman. She could have had any man.*

The arrival of the taxi interrupted her thoughts. The driver noticed Cindy's exhaustion and he helped her load her three bags in the trunk. When he asked her destination, she simply said, "Hilltop Police Department."

* * *

Agatha sat with Torianna in the kitchen, deep in conversation. "You should've seen Jonas the other night, my dear. He was terrified that there was a murderer in town."

Unsure how to react, Torianna watched her grandmother tell her story. She had also heard the gossip in town, and she knew there was a possibility of truth to the rumors. She chose not to tell her grandmother about the glove they examined at the lab. Nick asked her not to discuss their suspicions with anyone. Torianna knew her grandmother would not feed into the town gossip, but she did not want to worry her anymore than necessary, either.

"He was really worried?"

"You better believe it. I had a hard time trying to calm him down. I wouldn't let him leave until I knew he was thinking clearly."

"That's good." Torianna responded, reaching for a piece of banana nut bread.

"He's a real piece of work."

"Yes, he is."

"So," Agatha remarked, you never did give me any details about your little escapade with Nick."

"Escapade? Is that what you're calling it?"

"Yes. Well?"

Not trying to conceal the blush creeping up into her cheeks, Torianna said, "We had a good time."

"Now, dear, I know you talked about something. You were out there a long time."

"We talked... about a lot of things. And he asked me," she was cut off.

"...to marry you!"

"No. And I don't like how you're assuming," Torianna teased.

"I love you, that's why. Indulge me, what did he ask you?"

"I was trying to tell you." Torianna chuckled at her grandmother's antics. She continued, "He asked me, and he was pretty convincing too, to stay in Hilltop and work for him."

Agatha clapped her hands together. "I knew it! I knew you two would get together."

"We're not together, Grandma. I'll just be working for him and living with you," she made a joking face. "Hope you are looking for a roommate."

"There's still hope. He's going to ask you soon. And I'm happy to have you stay here. This is your home, too."

"And how do you know 'there's still hope'?"

"I just know. So, you're going to have to put up with me now?" she teased.

"Yeah, I don't know how I can live with that."

Their excited voices filled the kitchen.

* * *

Detective Daniels flipped through his copy of the case file pertaining to the investigation of the death of Sherry Wilkins. The results of the lab tests done on the rubber glove pleased him. But that still did not give him enough cause to get a search warrant for Darren Wilkins' property. The blood on the index finger of the glove proved a match to that of Sherry's blood. The lab technician found latent prints inside the glove, which belonged to Darren Wilkins. However, Daniels remained uncertain that a judge would view this evidence as probable cause for a search warrant. He was not even sure what to look for. The Ident technician canvassed the entire crime scene, but had not found anything unusual.

You may think you won, Darren, but I'm coming after you. Mitchell recognized his emotions meddled with his focus in this investigation. He loved Sherry, and now she was gone...because of Darren Wilkins. Mitchell perceived a potential problem of over-involvement, cause for the chief to remove him from the case. And he did not want that. He wanted to be the one to nail Darren Wilkins.

The officer at the front desk spoke over the intercom, "There's a lady here to see you, Detective Daniels."

Mitchell racked his brain, trying to figure out if he had an appointment. "Who is she?"

"Don't know, but she says it's important...that she has something you might want to see."

"Okay, you can send her in."

As Mitchell pondered who came to see him, a petite brunette approached his desk. She looked a bit out of sorts in this surrounding. He rose from his desk and offered her his hand. "Detective Daniels, ma'am."

She took his hand, "Cindy Johnson."

"Pleasure to meet you, Ms. Johnson. How can I help you?"

Cindy shifted in her seat, thankful that the taxi driver promised to wait fifteen minutes with her bags still in his car and that the Detective had been in. Not knowing who to ask for, she mentioned the Wilkins case, and the officer at the front desk directed her to Daniels. "I have something you might like to see." She fished around in her purse and handed him the disc.

Hesitant, but curious, Mitchell, accepted the disc. *What was this, some kind of game?*

Cindy interrupted his thoughts. "Maybe I should explain who I am first"

"That would be helpful." Daniels laid the disc on his desk. Cindy stared at it, fearing the Detective's papers might swallow the disc she'd risked her life for...the disc she knew Mrs. Wilkins had died for.

"I work for Mr. Wilkins, or I, uh, used to. I kinda left this morning. He has no idea because he went out of town."

At the mention of Wilkins' name, Mitchell's ears perked up. *This girl may have some juicy information.* "What did you do for Mr. Wilkins?"

"I worked as his housekeeper. He treated me more like servant. Not Mrs. Wilkins. She was a saint compared to him." Mitchell thought of Sherry and silently agreed. *She was a saint.*

"So why'd you leave?"

"He attacked me yesterday."

"Did he assault you, sexually?" He tried to ask this as sensitively as possible. "Maybe I shouldn't be the one you need to talk to. I'd better get a female officer over here."

The young woman spoke frankly of the incident. "He grabbed me in the kitchen. His hands were all over me. It was disgusting. You're probably thinking that I let him touch me, but I didn't. I tried to struggle away, but he held on so tight and I was scared. I don't get scared easily, but he scares me." She leaned forward. "I'm scared because I know he killed Mrs. Wilkins."

Mitchell grew hopeful. "You witnessed the murder?"

"No, but he did it." Mitchell tried to relax and let the girl finish with her story. "Mr. Wilkins asked me to start cleaning out his wife's wardrobe the day after she died. I thought that was suspicious. He was so cruel. He didn't even seem upset about her being shot to death. Even if it was a suicide, and he wasn't the murderer, he should've been upset, don't you think?"

Mitchell smiled at her logical thinking. "Yes, I agree."

"Anyway, I was cleaning her closet, finishing up and I found that disc. I'm sure there's something on the disc that Mrs. Wilkins didn't want her husband to see. Why else would she hide it?"

The young woman held Mitchell's full attention. "Right when I hid the disc in my apron, he came in the room and grabbed one of her negligees out of her dresser. His hands touching it made me so sick. I hate what he did to Sherry, I mean Mrs. Wilkins." Mitchell caught her use of Sherry's given name and knew the girl really cared for her employer.

"He tossed the silk on the bed and said...oh, never mind."

Mitchell saw the fear in the young woman's eyes as she told her story. *Fortunately, that jerk didn't hurt her.* He inspected Cindy as she spoke and realized that a grown woman, probably in her mid-twenties, sat in front of him. The officer at the front desk came into the back room and called loudly, "Hey, there's an impatient taxi driver out there. Any of you know about it?"

"Oh, my God," Cindy rose, grabbing her purse, "what time is it?"

"Ten-thirty."

"It's been more than fifteen minutes."

"Are you going somewhere?"

"No, but my bags are in the car."

Mitchell nodded, perceiving her situation. "I'll come outside with you and we'll go somewhere where we can talk."

He moved away from his desk. "The disc," she stopped him. He looked at her blankly. "Don't forget the disc. Mrs. Wilkins wanted us to find this. I just know it."

Mitchell grabbed the disc and followed Cindy out to the hall. *She certainly makes a lively first impression.*

* * *

"Hi, may I speak to Captain Elway, please?"

"I'm sorry, ma'am, he's busy right now."

"Tell him Detective Silverman would like to speak with him?"

"Oh, Detective, why didn't you say it was you? Hold on, a sec."

Torianna twisted the phone cord in her hand, unsure what to say to the Captain. Agatha pointed out to Torianna earlier that the 'Captain Superior' expected her back at work on Monday and now she wouldn't be there. Torianna smiled when she remembered Agatha's words. *So I think you have some explaining to do, young lady.*

"Hello, Detective," Captain Elway said.

"Captain, how are you?"

"I'm fine, Silverman. But I get the feeling I'm not going to like this. C'mon, out with it."

"I'm resigning."

Torianna heard his sharp intake of breath. *Oh, boy, I didn't think this was gonna be hard. Nick should be making this call.* "Captain, are you all right?"

"I'll get over it."

"Over it, sir?"

"I am losing the head of my Ident team. That's not something a captain wants to hear."

"I'm sorry, sir."

His tone was lighter. "You must have your reasons."

"Yes, sir, I do."

"Just get it to me in writing. Am I to assume this is in effect immediately?"

"Yes, sir. I'm sorry I couldn't give you more notice, but my circumstances…" he didn't let her finish.

"When are you cleaning out your desk?"

"I can't say for sure."

"Don't be a stranger, Silverman."

"I won't, Captain."

"Silverman?"

"Yes, sir?"

"You were one of the best detectives this department's ever had."

"Thank you, sir."

They said their good-byes and hung up.

* * *

Mitchell helped carry Cindy's luggage to his car and then he drove to the diner on Main Street. They chose a table by the window and sat down. Their waitress came by.

"I'll have a coffee. No cream or sugar."

"What about you, miss?"

"Decaf tea, please."

"So, where were we?" Mitchell smiled at his companion.

"The disc. So, what do you think is on it?"

"I don't know. But I think it's important."

"Why do you say that?"

"Because she obviously hid it from Mr. Wilkins."

"I suppose you could be right."

"Well, when can we check it out?"

"We?"

"Yes, I found it and I want to help. I cared about Mrs. Wilkins, and what he did to her…"

"I understand that, but I'm the detective, not you."

"Then give the disc back to me."

"I can't do that."

"Really? What if I take it back?"

"Look, I have the disc now and it's police evidence."

"Great," she huffed in frustration.

He leaned his arms on the table and stared at her. "Listen to me, miss. I knew Sherry too, a long time ago. I cared about her, okay? So I know how you feel."

His words silenced Cindy. The waitress returned with their order then. *At least I got the disc to the police and told my story. Guess I'm outta here, even though I have nowhere to go. I can't go back home. If I show my face there, Dad'll kill me. I'd rather sleep out on the street.*

"Hello?" Mitchell waved his hand in front of her face.

"Huh?"

"I asked if you had some place to go?"

Cindy put up her defense walls then, not wanting the police officer to pity her. She had told him enough "What difference does that make?"

"I just want to be sure you have somewhere to go."

She averted her eyes and admitted quietly, "I have nowhere to go. There, I said it, are you happy?" She quickly grew defensive.

"Why would I be happy?"

"I don't know. I'm sorry. It's been a long morning and yesterday was a nightmare. This whole weekend's been a nightmare."

"Look at me."

"What?"

"Look at me." She reluctantly obeyed.

"I believe your story and I want to help you, okay?"

She nodded, thankful that he trusted her.

He paid the bill and they walked out to his car. "Where are we going?"

"I know someone you can stay with for a while."

He opened the door for her and then went around to his side. "Hey, Cindy," she looked up sharply at his use of her first name, "how long is Mr. Wilkins going to be away?"

"A few days."

"Good, that's all the time I need."

Cindy shrugged her shoulders, not knowing what he meant, just glad to be in a car, far away from Mr. Wilkins and his house.

I've got you, Darren. All I need now is the search warrant. For the first time in a few days, Mitchell's spirits rose.

Chapter Fourteen

Finished with dinner, Torianna curled up on the sofa with her cat, Prints, when the phone rang. Agatha left earlier for a church prayer meeting. Torianna had to get up to answer the phone. She considered letting it ring. *But it could be Nick,* she thought hopefully.

"Hey, Red," Nick spoke loudly into the phone.

"You sound happy."

"I am. We've got great news."

"You and who else?"

"Remember I told you about Detective Daniels?"

"Maybe, I can't recall."

"He got Judge Warner to sign the search warrant." His excitement made her smile.

"Slow down. Search warrant for what? You're forgetting that I'm not up to speed on your case."

"You'd better start, because tomorrow's your first day of work."

"Really? Tomorrow's Saturday."

"Didn't I tell you there'd be crazy hours?" he laughed.

"Okay, what's my assignment, Mr. Coroner?"

"Well, Deputy, you get to show off your fingerprinting expertise."

"Sounds stimulating," Torianna remarked, actually getting excited. "But what about our date?"

"Don't worry, this won't take long. Our date's still on."

"I was settling in to read just when you called. Now I still can't read because I need to check my powder and supply of evidence bags and…"

He cut in. "I think you can manage, Red."

They said their good-byes. Torianna's inquisitive nature perked up. She really did miss work. *At least, now, I get to work with my favorite person.*

* * *

"It's about time you got here. I've been waiting for an hour. I was about to leave."

"Sorry about the delay. Traffic." Darren mumbled. He walked over and shook his partner's hand.

"So, is everything set?"

"Yes, I checked the warehouse myself before I left."

The man leaned against a wooden crate. "I heard about your little trouble."

"News flies fast these days."

"What'd you expect? You're the damn Mayor. Once the news snatches this up, they'll never let you rest."

"What are you talking about?" Darren asked, unruffled. "The coroner ruled it a suicide. There's nothing for me to worry about."

"I hope you're right. The way I heard it, the town's waiting to string you up."

Darren ignored the gossip and the horrible truth behind it. "It's not that bad."

"Not that bad! Darren, you killed your damn wife."

"She was getting in the way."

"So that's all there is to it? Eliminate whoever gets in your way?"

Darren's tone grew colder. "Listen, Randolph, I would shut up if I were you. You are my business partner, not my keeper, okay?"

Randolph caught the warning in his words. He remained silent, returning Darren's cold stare. "Fine, but don't say I didn't warn you."

Darren began pacing the room, and then turned quietly. "Now that you're aware of my feelings about this incident, maybe we can get down to business."

"That's all I ever want to be involved in, Darren. I won't be implicated in your mess."

Darren waved away Randolph's fear. "No problem. There won't be any more inquiries into the situation. You don't have to worry."

Darren opened his briefcase and handed Randolph an invoice of the shipment his driver needed to pick up from the warehouse. They stood by the desk and discussed the plans for several more minutes.

After their brief meeting ended, Darren clapped a hand to Randolph's back and asked solicitously, "Let's go grab a beer." Randolph, more relaxed with the incident lodged in the back of his mind, laughed amiably and led the way.

* * *

Cindy came down the stairs and hesitated at the landing before disturbing her hostess. She looked so comfortable on the sofa, engrossed in a novel, her cat purring on her lap. But Cindy needed to talk to someone, not wanting to sit upstairs in the guest bedroom all by herself.

Detective Daniels knew Agatha from church and he came to her with his strange request to let a young woman stay in her home. Always gracious, as he knew she would be, Agatha accepted Mitchell's new friend. Agatha thought it might be nice for Torianna to have another female her age in the house.

Torianna sensed someone's eyes on her and smiled her welcome when she saw Cindy standing in the hallway. "Hello. Come and sit down."

Cindy wrung her hands, "I'm not really used to living in a big house and actually being able to sit down and enjoy myself. I feel like I should be cleaning up."

Mitchell briefly explained Cindy's situation to Agatha and Torianna. "You don't have to clean up here. Make yourself at home." Torianna put her bookmark in place and laid the novel on the table. When she moved, Prints stretched his body and jumped off. "Sorry, little guy. Didn't mean to disturb your sleep," she scratched under his furry neck.

The cat walked over to Cindy and stuck his nose by her hand. "What's your cat's name?" she asked, stroking his back. The cat purred.

"Name's Prints."

"Oh, I get it. That's because you do fingerprints, right?"

Torianna looked shocked and then started laughing.

"What? Did I say something wrong?" Cindy asked, dumbfounded.

"No, you're the first person who ever understood my cat's name right when I said it."

"Huh?"

"People think I say P-R-I-N-C-E instead of P-R-I-N-T-S."

"That could be confusing," she replied, giggling.

"Actually, I called him Prints because he kept digging in my flower pot and walking the dirt all over my apartment, the floor, carpets, furniture, everything."

"So, it was keep the cat and get rid of the plant."

"Bingo."

Torianna and Cindy surprised themselves by this instant camaraderie. Neither of them had many friends. Torianna was so busy with work and Cindy was cooped up in the big house all the time, except when Mrs. Wilkins gave her permission to go to town.

Agatha came home in the meantime, after dropping Jonas off at his house. She poked her head into the living room to say hello, happy to see the two young women deep in conversation. She brought them some cookies and hot cocoa, then she walked up the stairs tired and ready for bed. *Now I'm going to have to bake more desserts,* she sighed, but there was a smile on her exhausted face.

* * *

The conversation turned more serious when Torianna mentioned her fingerprint work at the Wilkins' house tomorrow. In her initial excitement, she forgot Nick's warning not to talk to anyone about it. Cindy seemed interested and wished her luck finding anything that could put that man in jail. "I'm sorry about what happened to you," Torianna said quietly.

Cindy had to think a moment about what Torianna was referring to. She enjoyed herself so much tonight that she had almost forgotten about her experience. Well, not fully forgotten, but hopefully hidden somewhere far in the recesses of her mind. She had no desire to think about it. "Thank you. I'm sorry too. But I'm glad nothing worse happened. I would've been..., I don't know what I would've done...probably tried to kill myself. It was a nightmare that whole week. One I won't soon forget."

"I shouldn't have asked you."

"No, that's okay. You meant well."

"You know, I'm really tired. I'm gonna head to bed. You're welcome to stay down here if you'd like."

"No, you're right. It is kinda late."

Torianna checked her watch. "Wow we've been talking for a long time." She stood up and reached for her book. "I think you should come with us tomorrow." Prints sat up at attention, waiting for his mistress to head upstairs to bed. He always slept curled up in a little ball of fur on her feet.

Cindy looked surprised. "Me?"

"If it won't be too hard..."

"No, it's not that. I don't think Detective Daniels would let me. When I asked him about the disc, he said he was the cop and he could handle it."

Pensively, Torianna sighed, "Hmm. That's it," she exclaimed. "I'll convince Nick, he's the county coroner, to let you come. After all, you know the house better than any of us and you could help us get done a lot faster."

"I like that idea," Cindy said, warming up to the opportunity to help them. They both walked upstairs and went to their rooms to prepare for bed.

* * *

The moon cut into the darkness, creating a path of light from the window to the darkened form across the room. His arms hung listlessly on the arms of his chair; his legs sprawled out in front; his head hung down to his chest. A cat screeched outside near the window and the man jolted out of his slumber, knocking his shot glass over; amber liquid mixed with broken glass. He stumbled to his feet. As he walked towards his desk, he crossed paths with the moon's light. He shielded his eyes, grumbling.

The man grabbed the black and white photographs from the file and spread them on his desk. He leaned close and stared at the grotesque images confronting him. He roughly pushed the photographs aside and slid them into a drawer. In his intoxicated state, his actions betrayed his usual precautions. He left the photographs in the drawer, unprotected, and walked out of the room, bumping into furniture. The light of the room slowly disappeared as he closed the door.

Chapter Fifteen

Torianna and Cindy walked out of Agatha's house carrying the evidence collection kit to Detective Daniel's waiting car. Nick got out and opened the trunk for them. Torianna and Cindy got in the back seat and Nick went to the front passenger side. "What's this?" Mitchell asked, motioning towards Cindy.

"She's coming with us," Torianna said with as much authority as she could muster. She poked Nick on the shoulder, giving him a message with her eyes, asking for help.

"Um, we all thought Cindy should come with us, to help with the search."

"What does she know about police work?"

"Nothing, but she knows the house," Torianna piped up.

Mitchell looked in the rearview mirror and saw her sitting quietly. "Fine. But you better not get in the way," he almost growled. *Why am I giving her such a hard time? She had the guts to defend herself against a man like Wilkins and she waltzed right into the police department and told her story. Oh, I can't forget the disc.*

Mitchell put the car into reverse and drove out of the driveway.

* * *

They arrived at the Wilkins' house a few minutes later. Out of mere formality, since they knew he'd most likely be out of town, they knocked on the door. There was no answer and Detective Daniels was going to kick the door in. "Wait," Cindy stopped him, her hand lightly on his arm; "I forgot to give my key back," she handed the key to him.

He smiled politely and was going to place it in the keyhole, but she stopped him again. "It's for the back door. I wasn't allowed to come in the front entrance." Mitchell looked at the small brunette beside him and didn't like this protective feeling he was having for her.

"Okay, let's go to the back," he barked his order. Torianna smiled at Cindy and whispered that she shouldn't take his irritation personally.

They walked across the expansive lawn and veered to the side of the house. Cindy turned her head up and stared at the big white house. She had called this house her *home* for one year, but it hadn't seemed like a home to her. She was just thankful that Mrs. Wilkins had been kind and understanding.

Mitchell put the key into the hole and turned the lock. It opened and he placed the key in Cindy's palm. He told everyone to be quiet and not to touch anything until Torianna set the ground rules. None of them had been part of an Ident crime scene search before.

Torianna stepped into the back room and expected Mr. Wilkins to come out at any moment and chase them all out of his house. *Be reasonable and calm down. You can't let them see you afraid. Besides, you know what you're doing and can do it well.* "We've got to do this quickly. We don't know when the suspect is coming home. We're here legally, but we wouldn't want him to catch us. I don't think he'd be too happy. Since this is no longer a crime scene, we had to get a search warrant," she directed her statement to Cindy, knowing the other two officers would already be aware of this. She turned to Detective Daniels, "Did you get the whole house listed on the warrant? What about the grounds?"

"Judge Warner must have been having a good day, because he read my affidavit and search warrant, thought our case was probable, and signed the warrant. I didn't give him time to change his mind. I grabbed the papers and left."

"Okay," Torianna became Detective Silverman, Ident Officer, in full charge of the situation and ready to collect some evidence. "We should split up. Nick and I will check the house and you and Cindy check the grounds and any sheds. I brought gloves for everyone to wear. Remember, don't touch anything and write everything down." She handed a pad and pencil to Cindy. "Check what you see with any of the photos the police took on first examination. If you note any important difference, which it's obvious there may be some, write them down. If you think you found something that needs to be dusted for prints, put it in the evidence bags, packaged separately, and labeled. I like to print small items on the scene and then transport them. If the item is too big to be moved, come get me." She handed Cindy the photograph of the rubber glove. "We're looking for the other glove. Nick found this one near the driveway. Should we meet back in an hour?" she looked at Mitchell.

"Sounds good." He motioned for Cindy to follow him.

Nick whispered in Tori's ear, "I like it when you're in your *in charge mode*."

She smiled and they started through the house.

* * *

"We might be too late to get any prints," Nick said from his bent position on the floor.

"Not necessarily. Cindy couldn't possibly have cleaned every spot in this house where we might find something."

Torianna and Nick were in the kitchen. They had decided to start the search there for obvious reasons. The murder occurred in that room. Torianna put her kit on the table. "I have an idea, but I need your help." Nick stood up, listening. "When would you say the murder happened?"

"Early in the morning, a little bit after one."

"If we've established that he shot the victim, then she wouldn't have collapsed to the floor on her own. He could have carried the body."

"That's right. So, she could've been shot in any part of the house and brought to the kitchen. But why the kitchen?"

"Unless it happened in the kitchen. She'd still have to be moved a little. Most likely he wouldn't have been able to lay her body down on the exact spot she might have fallen if she shot herself."

"Yeah, I got you."

"So, try it on me."

"What?"

"Pretend you're the suspect and I'm the victim. Say I was down here in the early morning hours. Now why would I be down in the kitchen, if I was not planning to kill myself?"

"Probably getting a drink."

"Good. Maybe we're onto something. So she comes down to the kitchen, wearing what?"

"She had on a silk robe and slippers. Yeah, I remember that."

"She goes to the cabinet," Torianna moved forward, going through the motions, but refraining from touching anything, "takes out a cup and maybe leans against the counter or faces the window, her back to the kitchen entrance. The suspect comes into the room. Go ahead, pretend you're coming in. Now what do you do?"

"I don't know. Maybe I make my presence known, like I want to warn her and see her squirm."

"Umm. So she turns around or has already seen him come in. I tend to think that she was looking out the window. That's what I would be doing. Anyway, she sees him and almost spills her drink."

"Yeah, and then puts it down."

"The suspect would probably be coming towards her. Now we know he was wearing rubber gloves. Did we check the revolver for prints?" she asked suddenly.

"I don't know what our Ident officer did."

"We have to find out. Because his prints could have gone through the glove. Both of their prints might be on the gun. He most likely would've come up behind her. The slug entered on the right temple, correct?"

"Yeah. Got lodged in her skull."

"So come here and grab me like you think the suspect grabbed the victim." Nick shrugged his shoulders and came behind Torianna and took her in his arms. He really wanted to kiss her, but he knew she'd get mad. *not now,* he could hear her saying. He held his right forefinger and thumb in the form of a gun to her right temple. Just then footsteps sounded behind Torianna and Nick and startled them. Nick almost spun around, causing Torianna to loose her balance. She was about to reach out to the refrigerator when Nick steadied both of them.

Mitchell and Cindy walked into the room, their faces showing their surprise at the stance they'd found their partners in.

Nick stammered, "We, uh, we we're trying to re-enact the murder."

"Really?" Mitchell teased.

"I've got it," Torianna exclaimed. "I think I know where we can find prints."

"Where?" Nick asked excitedly.

"On the refrigerator door."

Mitchell looked at the fingerprint expert as if she'd lost her mind. "The what? You know how many times that's been handled?"

"Yes, I do. Just wait a second. Cindy, could you open the door how you normally do." She looked at Torianna skeptically; before she was told not to touch anything. "Go ahead."

Cindy reached out hesitantly and grabbed hold of the long black handle. Torianna was sure that's where the young woman would touch the appliance. "Did you ever notice Mr. or Mrs. Wilkins touching it any other way?"

By now, all three of them were looking at Torianna strangely. *How else are you supposed to open the door,* Mitchell thought. "They opened it the same way." She raised her eyebrows.

"Just hold on. There is a point here. Cindy, one more question, did either Mr. or Mrs. Wilkins have an annoying pet peeve of always keeping the appliances clean, free of fingerprints?"

Cindy thought for a moment. "Yes, as a matter of fact, Mrs. Wilkins liked to keep everything clean, in the kitchen, especially."

"So, it's safe to say that her hand prints would not be on the refrigerator door?"

"Most likely not. She was always wiping the appliances."

"Would you be willing to testify in court to that fact?"

"Torianna, what is this?" Mitchell looked impatient.

"I'm almost there. When we were startled by your entrance to the room, Nick practically turned me around, and I lost my balance, reaching out to the nearest object."

"The refrigerator," Nick said in amazement.

"Yes. Mrs. Wilkins would have experienced the same kind of imbalance and reached out for the closest available stability point. I believe there are patent palm prints on this door."

"But what does this prove?" Cindy questioned.

"That the victim was assisted in her suicide, if you get my meaning." She opened her kit and pulled out a flashlight. She pointed the light in several directions and saw the patent, visible under the light at just the right angle. She twirled the handle of her brush between her palms, fluffing out the bristles. Dipping the tip of the brush into the powder, Torianna brushed the dust lightly onto the print. Her captivated audience watched as she worked magic to make the prints appear. She brushed carefully in the direction of the print and blew some of the excess powder away. She took her pressure-wound tape from the evidence kit and pressed the tape down carefully, so as not to let any air get between the tape and the print. She pressed down hard on the print with her thumb. In one motion, she lifted the tape from the door, like tearing a band aide off her arm in one swipe to ease the agony of pulling it off little by little. She asked Nick to lay out the fingerprint lift card and she pressed the tape down in one motion on the edge of the card. She cut the tape from the roll and scribbled a rough sketch of where she found the print on the card and signed her initials to the top of the card. She asked Nick to sign his name as a witness to her work.

Cindy looked at Mitchell, pleased with their work. "We found a dark shirt, which I know belonged to Mr. Wilkins because I used to do their laundry and it has blood spots on it."

Torianna smiled at the group. Her new Ident team passed their first test. They searched around the house for other items of interest, but found nothing more after an hour. Detective Daniels decided that they should clear out. They made sure, even though they were not responsible to, that everything they touched was put back in place. They did not want to unnecessarily anger their suspect. He'd be angry enough when he found his copy of the search warrant, lying proudly on the kitchen table. *And won't he be surprised to see me gone.* Cindy smiled.

Torianna excused herself and went back into Mr. Wilkins' office; she had forgotten her bag. As she picked up her bag, she noticed something out of the corner of her eye. It was a folder and there were photographs sticking out. Curiosity overcoming her, Torianna opened the folder and peered at the photographs. *What is this?* Torianna's hand flew to her mouth, stopping the bile rising to her throat. *My parents? Why would he have pictures of them?* She stared at their lifeless forms, blood spilling out onto the floor, and Torianna fell to her knees and cried. She cried and heaved loud, aching sobs. Her heart began racing and her chest tightened. Her anxiety caused her breathing to grow heavy. She started shaking.

Nick came to the door and stopped. He ran into the room and picked up the photographs. He flipped the folder over and slammed them down on the desk in disgust. He put his arms around Torianna and helped her to her feet. "Let's get out of here," he whispered. Torianna's legs felt like lead and Nick had to help her stand to her feet.

She leaned heavily against his chest as his arm wrapped around her for support.

Chapter Sixteen

INVESTIGATION MADE INTO "SUICIDE"
DEATH OF MAYOR'S WIFE, NOW CALLED
A MURDER

Local - Yesterday, investigators'
search of the Mayor's house for
evidence has been linked to Mayor
Darren Wilkins. The investigation
is still pending.

* * *

Inside Walley's General Store, Wallace Reynolds leaned conspiratorially over the counter and spoke to his friend and store patron. "Did you read the paper?"

Dave Jenner answered in an equally hushed tone, but the other patrons in the store saw their close conversation and knew what they were discussing. The story stood out on the front page of the morning's paper. "It was interestin'," he replied.

"That's all you can say? I think the man should die for what he did."

"Keep your voice down, Wally."

"Why," he replied, "everyone in here knows what we're talking about. That Sherry, she was such a sweet thing. Don't know how she got mixed up with him."

A woman carrying her small child walked over to the counter in agreement. "I'm new to town and I didn't have a good feeling about the Mayor when I first met him at the town fair. How did he get elected?"

"Why, young lady," began the elderly grocer, "wasn't any one else on the ballot."

"No, that can't be. No one tried to run against him?"

"Ma'am, Darren Wilkins is the richest man in town. He's got his hands in things that no one wants to know about. Don't think ya'd want your husband going up against a man like that."

His dismal speech seemed to quiet the commotion in his store which soon might have turned into a rowdy town meeting. The young woman, with her child, paid for her purchases and exited the store, face set in consternation. She wondered if moving to this quiet little town from the city had been the right thing to do for her family.

Wally put his friendly grocer face back on as more people milled into his store. *I should probably keep my opinions to myself, before word gets out and I have to deal with Mr. Wilkins.*

* * *

Darren Wilkins arrived home earlier then planned. His business in the neighboring city was completed and he was just waiting for the driver to take his shipment away and make him a richer man than he already was. He drove his sedan up the long driveway.

When he pulled up in front of his house, nothing seemed out of the ordinary. He was glad to see that the little creature hadn't burned the house down. *Maybe she can keep house. Might be of use to me in the future. Need a wife if I'm to get re- elected. But then, again, no one will run against me.* He went straight for the front door, leaving his bags in the trunk. He could get them later. The front door was locked. *I wonder why she locked it. Probably afraid in this big house all by herself.* He put his key in the lock and opened the door. Inside, all was quiet. He walked through the downstairs, but didn't see his housekeeper anywhere. *Maybe she's upstairs. Even better.* Darren took the stairs two at a time. He didn't find his housekeeper anywhere on the second floor.

He ran back downstairs, his mind racing, and for the first time he felt the slightest twinge of fear that his plan was unraveling. He raced to her room at the back of the house and didn't even bother knocking. He pushed the door open. To his astonishment, she was not there. He checked her closet. All the clothes had been cleared out. Her drawers. Empty. The only sign of her was the uniforms that she had laid out on the unwrinkled bed. Duped again. Two females. *I didn't think she had it in her. Well, we'll see about this. You better not come crying back to me, honey.*

He went to the front door and looked for the morning paper. He reached down to the mat and picked up the plastic wrapped paper. He brought it to the kitchen and went to get something to drink. What he saw on the kitchen table made him drop his drink, shards of glass mixed with the orange liquid on the floor. *What's this?* He grabbed the paper and his horror mingled with his growing agitation. *A search warrant? What right did they have?* "I have nothing to hide. Let them search the whole damn house if they want to!" He shouted into the big empty house.

He threw the warrant on the table, not even bothering to clean up the mess. He had automatically left the spill and broken glass for his maid to clean up. He walked out of the house and went to bring his bags inside. *I have to do something about this.*

* * *

Agatha sat at her garden with her tools in gloved hands, humming quietly. She had just read the morning paper over her coffee and toast. She was a bit shocked at first, but then she had known along with the rest of the town that their Mayor was not the best example. *Here, I go again, always trying to be easy on people. Not the best example. He's far worse than that. He's as evil as the devil himself. He killed his wife. Tried to rape his housekeeper and is robbing this town blind of its funding. And we've been looking the other way and trying to figure out how our money gets spent. Who knows what else he's gotten his dirty hands into.*

Agatha knew their Mayor was bad news. But she didn't know what to do about it. Of course she could pray, but that was only her. She knew the Lord heard her prayers, but she wished for some type of togetherness in prayer. *Maybe I can get our prayer group at church to pray.* She raked back some loose dirt. *But what about Tori? She's part of this investigation.* Agatha knew she was a competent officer, the best, but that was when she was in New York. When she was home, she was a granddaughter and Agatha saw what was going on; it was a bit harder for her not to be so protective. She poured water on her bush and knew she'd have to leave her granddaughter in other more capable hands.

* * *

Darren stood inside his office, speaking on the phone. "What do you mean, there's nothing you can do?"

"I'm sorry, Darren, I knew this was gonna blow up in your face."

Darren was annoyed at the superior tone his partner had taken. "If I go down, what happens to your business then?"

"Trying to blackmail me?"

"No," Darren answered with a grin, "just giving you a warning."

"Look, I'd help if I could, but there's nothing I can do. I don't have any friends in your jurisdiction."

"We're still going ahead with the shipment?"

"Yeah. My driver will be there."

Darren hung up the phone and opened the window. He needed some air.

Chapter Seventeen

Inside Nick's lab, Torianna and Nick sat comfortably in the familiar surroundings. Detective Daniels and Cindy, on the other hand, were less comfortable. Torianna spoke about the print she had picked up and Cindy was busy staring around at the equipment and autopsy table. She didn't want to think about what happened on that table.

Detective Daniels touched her lightly on the arm, drawing her attention back to Torianna. "I called the forensics lab in New York and asked if we could bring the bloody shirt for examination. Nick and I have to leave as soon as possible. I checked the prints on the lift card with those of the victim's on file. The prints matched."

"Cindy and I can try to figure out the information of this disc."

"Really?" Cindy asked, excited.

They discussed their plan of action and quickly left for their destinations.

* * *

Agatha sat in her gazebo with her Bible study group. In agreement with Agatha's concerns for the town, when she suggested their group pray, they all readily came together.

They turned in their Bibles to the passage Agatha read. *Trust in the Lord and do good.* Their heads bowed in unison and their lips brought forth praises and pleadings up to the Heavenly Father of Lights. The presence of the Lord rested on the ladies. As they uttered their praises and prayed God's promises in His Word. Peace filled their hearts. They had an assurance that *the prayer of a righteous man is powerful and effective* and that they *could come boldly before God's throne of grace.*

* * *

They experienced a different drive to New York. They were both relaxed and communicating and there was no fear of meeting Phillip again. Tori would be free of any guilt if they did meet. She had even begun to hope, *maybe Nick does have feelings for me. But that's impossible.* She glanced sideways at Nick and stared at him long enough that he glanced at her. He looked questioningly and she shook her head in response. Nick turned his attention back towards the road, deftly maneuvering them through the traffic.

* * *

Detective Mitchell led Cindy through the hall towards the computer lab at the back of the department. He didn't want to be disturbed. He motioned for Cindy to take the seat beside his. He turned the monitor on and then the computer. "Do you know if their computer was IBM compatible?"

"No. I was never in the office when it was being used. I only cleaned it."

He hoped Sherry still used the Windows program she had on her own computer. He slipped the disc in the A drive and accessed the file in Windows. Mitchell's fingers moved over the keyboard, at times using the mouse. He had his work cut out for him, trying to find out which program she had used. He wasn't much of a computer wiz, but he knew enough. At least he hoped so.

* * *

Torianna and Nick strolled arm in arm through Central Park. After arriving and dropping the sealed evidence off at the forensics lab, Nick had suggested they spend some time in the park. Torianna agreed. She didn't want to be cooped up all day in her apartment. She knew she had to clean her desk out at work, but she planned to do that when they went back to check in with Janice.

Nick spotted an empty bench and led Torianna to it. They sat down and she snuggled against him. He rested his chin on her head. A companionable silence surrounded them. Torianna thought about everything that had happened in the past two weeks. Things had been exciting to say the least. "I hope we don't have any visitors," Nick joked.

"I know. I don't want to relive that day again. It's kind of scary to think that I almost married him."

"He wasn't that bad. Not compared to me."

"Not bad, I don't mean that. I just didn't love him. I realize that now. I think I was in love with love. God must have been watching out for me, even when I wasn't watching Him."

"But that's all behind you."

"Yes. I don't think I could marry any man I didn't love." She snuggled closer to his chest.

Nick wrapped his arm around her. *I hope you can love me someday, Red.* "Are you happy?" he asked suddenly.

She turned her head up, "Yes. I am, with you here."

"That's good." He smiled. "Do I get a reward?"

"Hmm. I don't know." She reached up and kissed him. *Yes, Red, I think that someday may happen real soon.*

* * *

Agatha rose from her seat and the ladies embraced one another, the joy of the Lord evident on each of their faces. Agatha led the ladies out of the gazebo and towards the house for some refreshment. She dropped back from the group, as they chatted ahead of her. *What joy is in my heart, Lord. I know you have heard our prayers. I feel your peace and I know your hand is over our town.*

* * *

Mitchell came back into the computer lab bringing a cup of tea for Cindy and coffee for himself. "Decaf tea for you."

"You remembered. Thanks."

He set his cup on the desk and turned back to the computer. "What I don't understand is, why would Sherry go through all the trouble of making this disc and not leaving any instructions for its use. How are we supposed to get inside her program?" He leaned towards the desk, his face in his hands.

Cindy watched him from her chair and smiled, happy that he let her come with him, and actually seemed to want her help. She had been quietly racking her brain, trying to figure out what Mrs. Wilkins was thinking. She could think of nothing. *Maybe this disc is nothing. Maybe she has her shopping lists on it.* She laughed.

Mitchell turned to look at her. "Why'd you laugh?"

"Oh, I was just trying to figure out what could be on this disc. And then I thought that it could be nothing, maybe just her shopping list. This might not be the lead you were looking for."

"Wait a minute," Mitchell sat back, turning his chair to face her. "Do you think this could be a shopping list?"

"I was just joking."

"No, I mean a list of the activities Darren was involved in, but labeled as a shopping list. You know, just in case Darren found the disc and checked into it."

"Sounds good, but why did he kill her?"

"Huh?"

"He probably killed her because he found the disc."

"Then why would he put the disc back?"

"I think he has the disc. We have a copy. He probably thinks that Mrs. Wilkins was not smart enough to make another disc."

"How can you be sure of that?" Mitchell asked, with interest.

"Because I saw how he treated her, like she was a child. He treated me the same way."

Mitchell regarded this with interest. *C'mon Sherry, what did you want us to do when we found it?* He turned back to the keyboard and said, "Keep talking about Sherry while I work at this. Think of anything you can remember that might help us get into her program."

* * *

Torianna led Nick to her desk in the Ident Unit. When she got there, Mahoney came forward, a big frown on his face, "Hey, Silverman, what's going on?"

"About?" Torianna hedged.

"You. You're leaving. Why?"

"I, uh, I'm going back home."

"I bet he had something to do with it," Mahoney said, pointing an accusing finger at Nick.

"That's not fair, John. It's not Nick's fault. It's time for me to move on."

Mahoney grunted and glared at Nick before he went back to his desk. "Johnson's in the back," he called over his shoulder.

"Who's Johnson?" Nick asked.

"Our newest Ident team member. Come back, I'll introduce you."

Torianna knocked on the door. Johnson called for her to come in. "Hello, boss," he grinned, "I hear you'll no longer be with us. Tired of this beautiful city?"

"Maybe. Time to move on."

"Who's this?"

"My friend and new boss, Nick Keyes."

"Ohh," he whistled, "the lady's gonna have her own boss now. You better watch out," he remarked to Nick, "she's a tough one. If you don't do what she says, she might just whip your butt."

"I've noticed," Nick joined in.

Torianna smiled and rolled her eyes. "I'll leave you two children to play. I've got a desk to clean out."

Torianna opened her drawers and started emptying the contents. Old case files. Sketch pads. A small 35mm camera. Books. Papers. Her hands grabbed onto the cold picture frame and she stared at his face. *Phillip. So confident. And happy. I wouldn't have made you happy. Phillip.* She wiped her hand over the glass and a tear splashed onto the picture. "I'm sorry," she whispered.

Nick came up behind her, knowing the face that stared back from the photograph. For a moment, he felt a twinge of jealousy; she was staring at Phillip's face a bit too long for Nick's comfort. *Cool it. It's understandable that seeing a picture of him might make her sentimental. It's not like he was a bad person, just not the right person,* and he smirked confidently.

Nick slipped his hands around her waist and leaned towards her ear. "Looks like you must've had fun working here. These guys are great, but I don't think Mahoney likes me very much."

Torianna put the photograph down on the desk, but didn't try to hide it from him. *That's a good sign,* Nick thought. His smile increased. *A little jealousy never hurt anyone.*

Torianna responded to his touch and caressed his cheek. "Yes, it was great working here. But I don't anymore and we shouldn't be doing this in front of everyone."

Nick glanced around the room and saw the guys half-looking and half-doing their work, pretending not to watch this display of affection. "Fine. But when we get out of here...," he let his voice trail off.

"When we get out of here, we have to check in with Janice and then head home."

Nick liked the way she said *home.*

* * *

"That's it!" Mitchell shouted, excitedly, "I think you've got it."

"What?"

"I think you've found the password."

"But I didn't say anything," Cindy remarked. They had been sitting in that room for hours. She had begun to think they would never get a breakthrough.

"It's what you didn't say. You were talking about how Sherry was unhappy with her marriage and she seemed like a trapped bird. So, I tried typing *black forest*, and we got in." He spun around in his chair and then kissed a surprised Cindy on her cheek.

He was too excited to deal with his nervousness around this young woman. He turned back to the computer. *I can't believe I just did that.*

Cindy, still in shock over his unexpected touch, said," Umm, what's this *black forest?*"

Mitchell stared at the monitor, avoiding Cindy's face. "It's a place where Sherry and I used to go, years ago." He wasn't thinking about Sherry this time, but about this attractive young woman behind him, who was chipping away at his walled up heart. "Why don't you move up," he suggested, "and we can try to open up the secret of this disc." Cindy's heart was beating too fast as she moved to sit closer to this man, who irritated her, yet amazed her the more she got to know him.

* * *

Down in the well-equipped forensics lab, Janice smiled at her guests. "You guys are in luck. The blood sample is a match with the first sample you gave on the rubber glove. I hope this bodes well for your case."

Torianna and Nick looked at each other, "Yes," Torianna said, "that's what we wanted to know." They thanked Janice for her assistance and left the lab. The blood on the shirt matched Sherry's blood found on the rubber glove. *Hopefully, Mitchell and Cindy have cracked the code and gotten into the disc,* Nick thought. He led Torianna towards his car.

The drive home was a silent one. There was no tension between Nick and Torianna, just a mutually agreed upon silence. Their thoughts were running in all directions; motives and theories collided with each other in Nick's mind. Torianna's thoughts were elsewhere. Her memories of the night of her parent's death were getting confused in her mind with visions of those photographs found in Wilkins' desk. She closed her eyes, squeezing them tightly, wishing she had no recollection of any of these memories. "Please go away," she whispered, her head leaning against the seat.

Nick turned his head in Torianna's direction; he saw her tightly shut eyes and turned his focus back onto the road. He had heard her whispered words. He kept silent and left her to her troubled thoughts.

Chapter Eighteen

Inside the vast white house, which stood cold and empty, Darren Wilkins stood in his bedroom and stared out the window. He called his lawyer earlier in the day, as soon as he found the search warrant, but his lawyer wasn't in. When he finally got in touch with him, his counsel hadn't been much help. He said the search was legally executed; whatever evidence the detectives found, would be admissible in court because they had properly listed the evidence to be searched for. Unhappy with this news, Darren grumbled his reply and hung up. As he walked to his liquor cabinet, he watched the wind blow through the trees. A storm was brewing.

* * *

Torianna called Mitchell at the police department in the off chance that he was still at work with Cindy deciphering the information on the disc. The officer at the front desk said that the Detective was in the computer lab. It was nine o'clock at night and the two of them were still in there. *I hope they found something,* Torianna muttered. Nick drove straight to the police department and they hurried into the computer lab.

They passed through the front desk and strode down the hall. When they got to the room, Torianna smiled. Detective Mitchell "no fun" Daniels was lounged out in the back with Cindy, both deep into a game of 500 rummy. Nick cleared his throat to announce their arrival.

Mitchell and Cindy stood up, almost bumping into each other, as if they were caught with their hands in the cookie jar. "Hey, guys," Mitchell said.

Cindy brushed a hand through her tousled hair. "Hello," she said shyly.

"So, did you crack the code?" Torianna asked excitedly.

"Yes, we did," Mitchell responded. He looked proudly at Cindy, "My partner here helped a lot. She kept telling me about Sherry, everything of importance she remembered her saying. That's how we stumbled onto the name *black forest.*"

"That's the code?" Nick asked.

"Yes, but we haven't figured out how Darren cracked the code."

"Why, do you think he had the disc and then put it back?" Nick asked.

"Because," Cindy answered, "he must've found the disc and then killed his wife because she knew too much. I'm sure this was the copy. Mrs. Wilkins was smart, smarter than Mr. Wilkins thought."

"What about you? Did the results come back?"

"Yes, Mitchell," Torianna replied, "you'll be pleased to know that the blood on the rubber glove matched the blood on the shirt, Sherry's blood."

Mitchell sighed in relief. He hoped the DA would listen to their evidence.

"What was on the disc?" Nick asked.

Cindy smiled, "We found loads of information from Darren's private bank accounts, his large deposits, and accounts of what he had been shipping."

"Was it drugs?"

"No, Tori," Mitchell answered, "it was computers, modems, fax machines. Everything you can imagine along the line of electronics, all shipped illegally out of state. We can get him on possession and selling of stolen goods, if nothing else."

"What are you saying?" Cindy asked.

"The murder charge may not stick. It's up the DA's office what they want to do with the charges."

"I can't believe this."

"Believe it, Cindy." Mitchell yawned and summed up the feelings of the entire group. "I think it's bedtime." They left their evidence, carefully sealed and labeled in the evidence locker and their case file, with the new information in Mitchell's desk. It had been a long day and they were glad to go home to bed.

* * *

The next morning, Mitchell rose early to get to work. He wanted to see Chief Roberts as soon as he got in. Detective Daniels hoped that the evidence they acquired would be enough to bring a case against Darren Wilkins, but he had his doubts. He kept thinking that just when he got close enough, Darren would get off the hook.

But the evidence had to be enough. It just had to. After what he did to Sherry and Cindy, if... he let his thoughts trail off and just sat at his desk. He wanted this whole thing finished. Rehashing this case only brought back his pain he'd felt in losing Sherry to Darren the first time. *Now, he'd lost her again when he hadn't really had her anyway.* His thoughts were spinning in confusion and his head was pounding. He needed some aspirin.

* * *

Inside Agatha's kitchen, Torianna sat pondering the meeting soon to occur between the Chief and Detective Daniels. She prayed the Detective would have the right words to say in presenting his case and that he wouldn't get too emotional over his lost friend. She plopped a grape in her mouth and whispered a soft thank you to the Lord for directing her path and bringing her home. She had no nightmares nor restless nights this past week. The painful memories of that night so long ago, embedded in her memory, were becoming less and less a part of her thoughts. She had started the process of facing up to her horrible fears, guilt, and anger that day Nick found her in Mr. Wilkin's office after she'd seen the photographs. She was grateful for that. She wanted to trust the Lord with her life, her future, and her heart.

She thought about Nick and wished he was here with her, sharing the bright sunny morning, eating grapes. She wondered how he really felt about her. Did he love her? She wasn't sure how she felt. But the mere mention of his name, or the image of his face in her mind, sent her heart racing. *Maybe that's a sign...*

She started humming and Cindy chose that moment to come down to the kitchen. She asked how Torianna slept that night. Cindy went to the cabinet and started to pour herself a bowl of cereal. When she came back to the table, Torianna noticed the preoccupation on her face.

"Are you okay?" Torianna asked.

"I'm fine, I was just wondering about Mitchell, I mean Detective Daniels."

Torianna tried to hide her smile. "I'm sure he's fine." She plopped another grape into her mouth. "He's handsome, isn't he?"

Cindy almost dropped her spoon. "I, uh, yes, I guess he is."

"It's okay to admit it."

"Admit what?"

"That you find the Detective attractive and maybe there's something more," she laughed.

"Oh, there's nothing more."

"You two seemed pretty cozy last night."

"He doesn't like me."

"I think he does."

Cindy laughed nervously and went back to her cereal; she blushed and Torianna thought Mitchell and Cindy would be a great match.

* * *

Nick got out of his car and went to his lab. He wanted to go over the reports one more time to make sure everything added up. They had searched through the case file yesterday and the prints from the gun. The prints were rubbed together and nothing definitive had shown up.

There has to be something I'm missing. He flipped through the file, not knowing what to look for. After a few minutes, he stood up and began pacing. *Come on, think. We got the blood stains checked. The revolver didn't help us.* Nick stopped pacing and looked through the case file. *That's it!* "Yes! I've got to get Tori in here now." He raced over to his phone and dialed the number he knew so well.

* * *

Torianna stood beside Nick in the lab. She had been interrupted from her conversation with Cindy and told to get to the lab immediately. Torianna had no idea what was so important. It was only eight o'clock in the morning. She didn't have to be at work for another hour yet.

"So, you're already starting with your bossiness?" Torianna questioned.

"I'm sorry that I ordered you to get here, Red, but I wanted to check this out before Mitchell talks to Chief Roberts."

"What's so important?"

"We forgot something."

"What?"

"Come here." He held up the suicide note.

She stared at it, not comprehending what he wanted her to see. "Red, look, it's been printed out from a computer.

"So."

"Have you ever heard of a suicide victim sitting down to the computer to type a letter before they shot themselves in the head?"

"No. I've usually seen handwritten notes."

"Exactly."

"What are you getting at?"

"Mrs. Wilkins didn't type this note. Her husband did and we can prove it."

"How?" Torianna sighed. It was too early for this game.

"Find the prints on the paper."

"Yes, you're brilliant. His prints are all over this paper. Unless, of course, he used gloves."

"But the prints could've gone through the gloves, remember, if they're thin enough."

Torianna quickly got to work. She would use Iodine fuming instead of spraying with ninhydrin, because then the prints could take up to twenty-four hours to develop. She used a blowpipe to breathe through the fiber glass filter over iodine crystals onto the paper. The prints developed quickly. Using her special fingerprint camera, she photographed the prints immediately. She finished her task. This was different than dusting for prints with powder because the iodine worked on the oils on the paper. The oils came from things people touched, such as the face, since prints don't produce their own oil. Nick was enlisted to finish the task so they could get to the Detective before he saw the chief.

Chapter Nineteen

Darren paced his office waiting for the phone to ring. He was expecting Randolph's call. His agitation grew as the hours passed and there was no phone call. Darren walked to his desk and picked up his glass; he sipped the brandy and thought about the money he would rake in from this shipment. After this deal was done, he would head for a southern vacation, maybe Mexico.

The phone finally did ring, startling him. He swirled the dark liquid in his glass, his other hand firmly grasping the phone. His nerves were acting up. His partner sounded different, not at all as worried as was his usual tone. Darren wasn't sure if that should bother him, but he was beginning to feel the effects of the brandy dulling his senses.

Randolph told him he wanted the shipment on its way tonight. Darren wondered at the change in plans. "That's a day early. What's going on?"

"Don't worry. Everything's going as planned. Just a slight change."

* * *

Torianna and Cindy were relaxed and lounging out in the gazebo at Agatha's house. All Nick and Mitchell had told them was that things were going according to plan and that they shouldn't worry. The DA was cooperating with them. Nick and Mitchell said to wait up for them because they had a surprise when they got to Agatha's house.

Torianna was excited about the suspense. She always liked surprises. Cindy, on the other hand, was a bit skeptical by nature and let Torianna have her excitement. *I'm not gonna get all worked up over nothing,* Cindy thought.

"Here you go, ladies," Agatha popped her head in the screen door. "I brought you some iced tea."

"No cookies?" Torianna teased.

"Nope," she set the tray down and sat heavily on the chair, "I had a very busy day. No time to bake any desserts for you."

"We'll forgive you," replied Torianna.

"Why are you in such a good mood?" Agatha asked.

"She's excited about some surprise the guys are bringing here, later."

"Ohh, a surprise. I love surprises."

"I thought you would," Cindy replied dryly.

Agatha took her cold drink and Torianna leaned back in her chair. "You know, this has been the busiest few weeks of my life."

"Mine, too," Cindy remarked.

"Aggie! Aggie!" a familiar voice called. Agatha stood up, as if on cue.

Torianna reached for her hand and laughed, sympathy in her voice, "We can hide you somewhere."

"No, I'll be fine. How late are you ladies going to be out here?"

Torianna looked at Cindy and shrugged. "They said to wait up for them. I don't know how late, but we'll be quiet if you want to go to bed."

Agatha sighed and shook her head. "I don't know if I'll be able to get to bed early, now." She laughed good-naturedly and walked back to the house, where Jonas waited excitedly by the back door.

Cindy smiled after Agatha's retreating form and said, "I'm so thankful your grandmother let me stay here."

"You're more than welcome. I know she would say that. Before Detective Daniels was done explaining your story, she offered her house."

Tears filled Cindy's eyes, "Thanks. I don't know what else to say."

"That's more than enough. I'm glad you're here. I hope you won't leave any time soon."

Cindy pulled her knees to her chest. "I don't know when I'll leave. I know it should be soon. I don't want to wear out my welcome."

"I don't think that will happen. My grandmother has this big old house to herself. She's been trying to get me to visit for a long time. Once I got here, I really didn't want to go."

"Is it also because of Nick?" Cindy asked shyly.

"Yes, it is. My feelings for him are puzzling. I'm not even gonna try to analyze them."

"You don't need to. Just go with how you feel. Your heart knows."

"You think so?"

"Yes, I do."

* * *

Darren somehow got to the warehouse to await his shipment. He was not drunk, but his head was spinning and he felt kind of groggy. He walked slowly towards the back of the building and opened the padlock with his key. When he finally got the door open, he went inside and shut the door behind him. He walked to the middle of the warehouse and looked around. Everything seemed normal to his blurred eyes, but something felt wrong.

The inside of the old building was still dark as usual. Darren saw the unopened crates. Nothing seemed out of place, but him. He was strangely disoriented, and not because of the alcohol. Something had come over him, a wave of confusion, and he wasn't sure if he would be able to get through the night without foiling his own plan. *My plan. But it's already been messed up. I shouldn't be here now.* He walked, trying to clear his head.

"No, Randolph said to be here tonight," Darren said out loud. "He called today. I'm not going crazy. I heard him. He said everything would be alright."

* * *

117

Nick sat in the unmarked police car with Mitchell. They had driven here with five other patrol cars, waiting for their prey to step into the trap. It was such a delicious trap that Mitchell could almost taste it. He was quiet and pensive when Nick interrupted his thoughts.

"Do you think this is going to work?"

"Why wouldn't it?"

"I don't know, I just want to get this guy."

"So do I." Mitchell peered into the darkness. They arrived a few minutes after Darren Wilkins got there. They saw his car parked in the back. The patrol cars were positioned around the building with back up on the way, if necessary.

"Do you think we really need this much back-up?"

"If we don't want him to get away, then, yes," Mitchell remarked, his calm tone coating over his agitation. He wished the truck would get there. Then Darren would be in jail and he could get on with his own life free of haunting memories. *And then what?* Images of a young brunette with a saucy temper flashed in his mind. He remembered their brief kiss. He hoped he hadn't scared her away. *She didn't seem to mind. We had a nice time playing cards.*

Nick interrupted his thoughts again. Mitchell was starting to get really tired of having Nick in the car with them on this stakeout. "What?" he growled.

Nick, unperturbed by his friend's moodiness, pointed in the direction of the coming headlights, "The truck. Let's get ready."

* * *

Inside the warehouse, Darren heard the tractor trailer coming to a grinding halt in front of the doors. He stood up from his crouched position on the floor and shook his head, trying to shake away his nagging fear and confusion. He walked to the door and lifted the latch. He started to pull the door open and then stopped.

The tractor's bright headlights shone on his face, blinding him. He held his hands up, trying to block out the harsh brightness. Randolph came in the warehouse then and greeted his partner.

"What's with the lights, Randolph? Trying to blind me?"

"No. Sorry about that. I've got a new driver. He's going to back the truck up and turn around so we can load it in here."

Darren waited for the truck to back up and then Randolph motioned for him to open one crate. "What for? Don't you trust me?"

"Yeah. But just humor me."

Darren moved to get the crowbar and he proceeded in opening the crate. He lifted off the wooden lid and showed Randolph the contents. He picked up a laser printer and handed it to Randolph. He motioned for Darren to put it back in the crate.

At that moment, spotlights shone in the warehouse and policemen surrounded Darren, closing in on him. A loud voice called, "Darren Wilkins, you're under arrest for robbery and possession of stolen goods. And," Detective Daniels stared down at his shocked face, "for the murder of Sherry Wilkins. Read him his rights." The Detective handed the suspect over to the officer standing at his side.

The officer rattled off the Miranda rights and led Darren away. The confused mayor turned his head and shouted, "What about him. He was in on it," he pointed to Randolph.

"Yeah, he was in on it," Detective Daniels said. "He came to us and plea-bargained for turning you in. And I mean, you're in now. For a long time."

Chapter Twenty

Torianna and Cindy were talking in the gazebo when they saw the headlights in the driveway. "They're here, Cindy."

I wonder what this is all about, Cindy thought.

Nick and Mitchell walked across the lawn towards the gazebo. Their faces hid the news, whatever it was.

"It's finally over," Nick practically shouted.

"What do you mean?" asked Torianna

"We caught him in the act, and it really was an *act.* Now he's off to the county jail."

"Are you serious?" Cindy hadn't expected great news like that. *Oh, Mrs. Wilkins, I'm so happy your memory is not tainted anymore. He's gonna get what he deserves.*

Mitchell and Nick pulled up chairs and Torianna offered to go get them some iced tea.

When she walked into the kitchen, Agatha was sitting at the table, reading her Bible. Torianna slipped happily into the room and placed her arms around her grandmother. "It's all over, Grandma."

"What are you talking about, dear?"

"The Mayor, Mr. Wilkins, he's been arrested."

"Oh, goodness," Agatha replied. "Oh, oh this is wonderful. Thank you for telling me dear." Torianna poured two glasses of iced tea. "I thought you'd be in bed. It's late."

"Now, listen here. I may be old, but I'm no invalid," she teased.

"Good night, Grandma, see you in the morning." She carried the two glasses outside, happy that justice would be served.

* * *

After the initial excitement wore off, Mitchell asked Cindy to go with him to a local coffee shop. Inside the gazebo, Nick's smile left. "What's wrong? Nick, you look sick."

"I have some awful news, Red. I wanted to tell you when you were alone."

"Nick, you're scaring me. What's going on?"

"Mitchell and I went with the officers to the station. He admitted to murdering your parents. I'm so sorry."

"What? Who?" Tori started breathing heavily.

"Darren Wilkins," Nick knelt down in front of Torianna and held her hands tightly. "He'd been involved in this mess for a long time, even before he became Mayor. Your father found out and...and you know the rest."

"He just told the Detectives this? I can't believe it. Why did the case get closed, no one ever helped my parents," she shuddered.

Nick pulled her into his arms and whispered softly, "They didn't have anyone to fight for them, Red. We fought for Sherry; they had no one."

"But I was there. I did nothing."

"You were just a child, Red. There was nothing you could do."

Torianna wiped her tears roughly with her hands. "I need to know the details."

"No. Not now. Let me hold you."

Torianna moved quickly into Nick's embrace as he whispered, "God will bring us through this."

"Us?" Torianna raised her head, hope in her eyes.

"Yes, us."

They rested together in each other's arms.

The warm air washed over them like the calm after the storm, such a soft breeze. It wafted into every open window in town, filling empty spaces with a warm awakening. In the night quiet, birds perched on tree branches in the solitude of the forest, the black forest, a place where two lovers went to feel free in the wind and knew such love. Their moment shattered by circumstances, a mere human powerless to change. The darkness came and the night swept blacker than the light, blocking out the hope. But the presence of peace cut through the darkness and brought a peace to this little town, a place of paradise, a place where God walks with those who seek his face, a shelter from the shadows.

Epilogue

Several Months Later

The lab was quiet. Nick had gone out to get lunch and Torianna decided to stay. She was backed up with some lift cards she had to search through to find matches and she wanted to get finished before she left work this afternoon.

Torianna wiped her forearm across her face and unknown to her, smeared fingerprint powder on her nose and forehead. She continued with her work, her hands dirty with the black powder. She had spilled the dust before and made a mess. She hadn't bothered cleaning up. The feel of the powder on her hands, and working in the lab, quenched her desire for adventure. She was extremely satisfied with her life. Working with Nick had turned out to be a bunch of surprises every day. They taught each other new things all the time. She felt fulfilled, except that she wasn't sure where she stood with Nick.

Sometimes she thought he loved her and other times she wasn't so sure that he wanted a long-term relationship. She certainly did; and like she said to Nick a few months ago, she could never marry a man she didn't love. *But she did love Nick.* She didn't know when it happened. Somewhere in the middle of her adventure, she fell in love with him.

Footsteps startled Torianna out of her reverie. She looked up and smiled when she saw Nick coming down the stairs with a bag. Lunch. She was starving. He saw the smudge of powder on her forehead and nose, but didn't say anything. He thought she looked cute, so busy at work, doing what she loved.

"Hey there, beautiful. What are ya up to?"

"Up to my elbows in powder, that's what. I must look a mess."

"You look wonderful."

"Really?"

In answer, Nick came over and hugged her. "Put your work down for a bit and come sit with me. You need to eat."

Torianna obeyed and watched as he took out a white tablecloth and spread it on the floor, followed by two champagne glasses, and grapes. He took out a wedge of cheese and some crackers.

"What is this?" Torianna laughed.

"Lunch." He smiled proudly.

"And the occasion is?"

"I'm just sharing a picnic lunch with my fair lady."

"Indoors?"

"The best kind."

Nick took out a single red rose and offered it to her. "Take it, it's my gift to the most beautiful lady in all the world."

She took the rose. She loved roses and she loved that he remembered that. She closed her eyes and held the rose close to her nose, inhaling its fresh fragrance.

Nick was glad that she had been distracted with the rose and closed her eyes. It gave him a chance to drop something into her champagne glass. He popped open the bottle and poured in the shimmering liquid, filling the glasses.

"You can open your eyes now."

She raised her eyebrows at his command. She kept her eyes open and looked down as he handed her the champagne glass. "Let's toast to us and our love for each other."

They raised their glasses, clinking them together, and then took sips of the champagne. Nick was surprised that she didn't notice the ring inside. *I guess I poured too much in.* "I think there's something floating in your glass. It's dirty or something."

"What? Thanks a lot," she joked. "Last time I'll trust you to pour my drink." The light caught on something shiny inside the glass. She had a sharp intake of breath. Her mouth hung open. "Oh, Nick."

He reached across his picnic blanket and took the ring out of the glass. He became a little nervous at this point and his hands were shaking as he wiped the ring off on a napkin. He held onto her left hand, stained with fingerprint powder and asked, "My dearest Red, will you marry me?"

"Yes. Yes, I will."

He started to slip the ring onto her finger. "But it's gonna get dirty."

"So, we'll wash your hands."

"The powder doesn't wash off easily."

"Do you have to be difficult about this?" he teased, "Johnson warned me about you." He slipped the ring onto her finger and reached out, pulling her towards him, his lips claiming her mouth.